Drown

Junot Díaz was born in Santo Domingo, Dominican Republic. He is a graduate of Rutgers University and received his Master of Fine Arts Degree from Cornell University. He teaches creative writing at MIT (Massachussetts Institute of Technology). His first novel, *The Brief Wondrous Life of Oscar Wao*, was published in 2007 to international acclaim and won both the Pulitzer Prize and the American National Book Critics Circle Award for Fiction. *The New York Times* described it as 'a book which decisively establishes Junot Díaz as one of contemporary fiction's most distinctive and irresistable new voices and *The Times* called it 'a masterpiece . . . its characters are unforgettable.'

'The language is a revelation, the very soul of a new identity . . . Junot Díaz definitely is a wonderful and unique talent. He's a natural.'
Francisco Goldman, *Observer*

'This stunning collection of stories is an unsentimental glimpse at life among immigrants from the Dominican Republic – and another front-line report on the ambivalent promise of the American dream.'
San Francisco Chronicle

'He's the latest overnight literary sensation. But luck had nothing to do with Díaz's success. He earned it with his talent . . . Díaz has the dispassionate eye of a journalist and the tongue of a poet, and when he sheepishly wishes aloud that his début had been way quieter, he's just wasting his breath. Talent this big will always make noise.'
Newsweek

by the same author

THE BRIEF WONDROUS LIFE OF
OSCAR WAO

THIS IS HOW YOU LOSE HER

Drown

Junot Díaz

faber and faber

First published in 1996
by Faber and Faber Limited
Bloomsbury House
74-77 Great Russell Street
London WC1B 3DA

Open market edition first published in 1997
This paperback edition first published in 2008

Typeset by Faber and Faber Ltd
Printed and bound by CPI Group (UK) Ltd, Croydon, CRO 4YY

© Junot Díaz, 1996

Junot Díaz is hereby identified as author of this work in accordance with
Section 77 of the Copyright, Designs and Patents Act 1988

A CIP record for this book is available from the British Library

ISBN 978-0-571-24497-3

10 9 8 7 6 5

Para mi comadre
Nicole Aragi

The fact that I
am writing to you
in English
already falsifies what I
wanted to tell you.
My subject:
how to explain to you that I
don't belong to English
though I belong nowhere else

Gustavo Pérez Firmat

Contents

Ysrael

1

We were on our way to the colmado for an errand, a beer for my tío, when Rafa stood still and tilted his head, as if listening to a message I couldn't hear, something beamed in from afar. We were close to the colmado; you could hear the music and the gentle clop of drunken voices. I was nine that summer, but my brother was twelve, and he was the one who wanted to see Ysrael, who looked out towards Barbacoa and said, We should pay that kid a visit.

2

Mami shipped me and Rafa out to the campo every summer. She worked long hours at the chocolate factory and didn't have the time or the energy to look after us during the months school was out. Rafa and I stayed with our tíos, in a small wooden house just outside Ocoa; rose bushes blazed around the yard like compass points and the mango trees spread out deep blankets of shade where we could rest and play dominos, but the campo was nothing like our barrio in Santo Domingo. In the campo there was nothing to do, no one to see. You didn't get television or electricity and Rafa, who was older and expected more, woke up every morning pissy and dissatisfied. He stood out on the patio in his shorts and looked out over the mountains, at the mists that gathered like water, at the brucal trees that blazed like fires on the mountain. This, he said, is shit.

Worse than shit, I said.

Yeah, he said, and when I get home, I'm going to go crazy – chinga all my girls and then chinga everyone else's. I won't stop dancing either. I'm going to be like those guys in the record books who dance four or five days straight.

Tío Miguel had chores for us (mostly we chopped wood for the smokehouse and brought water up from the river) but we finished these as easy as we threw off our shirts, the rest of the day punching us in the face. We caught jaivas in the streams and spent hours walking across the valley to see girls who were never there; we set traps for jurones we never caught and toughened up our roosters with pails of cold water. We worked hard at keeping busy.

I didn't mind these summers, wouldn't forget them the way Rafa would. Back home in the Capital, Rafa had his own friends, a bunch of tígueres who liked to knock down our neighbors and who scrawled chocha and toto on walls and curbs. Back in the Capital he rarely said anything to me except Shut up, pendejo. Unless, of course, he was mad and then he had about five hundred routines he liked to lay on me. Most of them had to do with my complexion, my hair, the size of my lips. It's the Haitian, he'd say to his buddies. Hey Señor Haitian, Mami found you on the border and only took you in because she felt sorry for you.

If I was stupid enough to mouth off to him – about the hair that was growing on his back or the time the tip of his pinga had swollen to the size of a lemon – he pounded the hell out of me and then I would run as far as I could. In the Capital Rafa and I fought so much that our neighbors took to smashing broomsticks over us to break it up, but in the campo it wasn't like that. In the campo we were friends.

The summer I was nine, Rafa shot whole afternoons talking about whatever chica he was getting with – not that the campo girls gave up ass like the girls back in the Capital but kissing them, he told me, was pretty much the same. He'd take the campo girls down to the dams to swim and if he was lucky they let him put it in their mouth or in their asses. He'd done La Muda that way for almost a month before her parents heard about it and barred her from leaving the house forever.

He wore the same outfit when he went to see these girls, a shirt and pants that my father had sent him from the States last Christmas. I always followed Rafa, trying to convince him to let me tag along.

Go home, he'd say. I'll be back in a few hours.

I'll walk you.

I don't need you to walk me anywhere. Just wait for me.

If I kept on he'd punch me in the shoulder and walk on until what was left of him was the color of his shirt filling in the spaces between the leaves. Something inside of me would sag like a sail. I would yell his name and he'd hurry on, the ferns and branches and flower pods trembling in his wake.

Later, while we were in bed listening to the rats on the zinc roof he might tell me what he'd done. I'd hear about tetas and chochas and leche and he'd talk without looking over at me. There was a girl he'd gone to see, half-Haitian but he ended up with her sister. Another who believed she

3

wouldn't get pregnant if she drank a Coca-Cola afterwards. And one who was pregnant and didn't give a damn about anything. His hands were behind his head and his feet were crossed at the ankles. He was handsome and spoke out of the corner of his mouth. I was too young to understand most of what he said, but I listened to him anyway, in case these things might be useful in the future.

3

Ysrael was a different story. Even on this side of Ocoa people had heard of him, how when he was a baby a pig had eaten his face off, skinned it like an orange. He was something to talk about, a name that set the kids to screaming, worse than el Cuco or la Vieja Calusa.

I'd seen Ysrael my first time the year before, right after the dams were finished. I was in town, farting around, when a single-prop plane swept in across the sky. A door opened on the fuselage and a man began to kick out tall bundles that exploded into thousands of leaflets as soon as the wind got to them. They came down as slow as butterfly blossoms and were posters of wrestlers, not politicians, and that's when us kids started shouting at each other. Usually the planes only covered Ocoa, but if extras had been printed the nearby towns would also get leaflets, especially if the match or the election was a big one. The paper would cling to the trees for weeks.

I spotted Ysrael in an alley, stooping over a stack of leaflets that had not come undone from its thin cord. He was wearing his mask.

What are you doing? I said.

What do you think I'm doing?

4

He picked up the bundle and ran down the alley, away from me. Some other boys saw him and wheeled around, howling but, coño, could he run.

That's Ysrael! I was told. He's ugly and he's got a cousin around here but we don't like him either. And that face of his would make you sick!

I told my brother later when I got home and he sat up in his bed. Could you see under the mask?

Not really.

That's something we got to check out. I hear it's bad.

The night before we went to look for him my brother couldn't sleep. He kicked at the mosquito netting and I could hear the mesh tearing just a little. My tío was yukking it up with his buddies in the yard. One of tío's roosters had won big the day before and he was thinking of taking it to the Capital.

People around here don't bet worth a damn, he was saying. Your average campesino only bets big when he feels lucky and how many of them feel lucky?

You're feeling lucky right now.

You're damn right about that. That's why I have to find myself some big spenders.

I wonder how much of Ysrael's face is gone, Rafa said.

He has his eyes.

That's a lot, he assured me. You'd think eyes would be the first thing a pig would go for. Eyes are soft. And salty.

How do you know that?

I licked one, he said.

Maybe his ears.

And his nose. Anything that sticks out.

Everyone had a different opinion on the damage. Tío

5

said it wasn't bad but the father was very sensitive about anyone taunting his oldest son, which explained the mask. Tía said that if we were to look on his face we would be sad for the rest of our lives. That's why the poor boy's mother spends her day in church. I had never been sad more than a few hours and the thought of that sensation lasting a lifetime scared the hell out of me. My brother kept pinching my face during the night, like I was a mango. The cheeks, he said. And the chin. But the forehead would be a lot harder. The skin's tight.

All right, I said. Ya.

The next morning the roosters were screaming. Rafa dumped the ponchera in the weeds and then collected our shoes from the patio, careful not to step on the pile of cacao beans Tía had set out to dry. Rafa went into the smokehouse and emerged with his knife and two oranges. He peeled them and handed me mine. When we heard Tía coughing in the house, we started on our way. I kept expecting Rafa to send me home and the longer he went without speaking, the more excited I became. Twice I put my hands over my mouth to stop from laughing. We went slow, grabbing saplings and fenceposts to keep from tumbling down the rough brambled slope. Smoke was rising from the fields that had been burned the night before, and the trees that had not exploded or collapsed stood in the black ash like spears. At the bottom of the hill we followed the road that would take us to Ocoa. I was carrying the two Coca-Cola empties Tío had hidden in the chicken coop.

We joined two women, our neighbors, who were waiting by the colmado on their way to mass.

I put the bottles on the counter. Chicho folded up yes-

6

terday's *El Nacional*. When he put fresh Cokes next to the empties, I said, We want the refund.

Chicho put his elbows on the counter and looked me over. Are you supposed to be doing that?

Yes, I said.

You better be giving this money back to your tío, he said. I stared at the pastelitos and chicharrón he kept under a fly-specked glass. He slapped the coins onto the counter. I'm going to stay out of this, he said. What you do with this money is your own concern. I'm just a businessman.

How much of this do we need? I asked Rafa.

All of it.

Can't we buy something to eat?

Save it for a drink. You'll be real thirsty later.

Maybe we should eat.

Don't be stupid.

How about if I just bought us some gum?

Give me that money, he said.

OK, I said. I was just asking.

Then stop. Rafa was looking up the road, distracted; I knew that expression better than anyone. He was scheming. Every now and then he glanced over at the two women, who were conversing loudly, their arms crossed over their big chests. When the first autobus trundled to a stop and the women got on, Rafa watched their asses bucking under their dresses. The cobrador leaned out from the passenger door and said, Well? And Rafa said, Beat it, baldie.

What are we waiting for? I said. That one had air conditioning.

I want a younger cobrador, Rafa said, still looking down the road. I went to the counter and tapped my finger on the glass case. Chicho handed me a pastelito and after putting it in my pocket, I slid him a coin. Business is business, Chicho announced but my brother didn't bother to look. He was flagging down the next autobus.

Get to the back, Rafa said. He framed himself in the main door, his toes out in the air, his hands curled up on the top lip of the door. He stood next to the cobrador, who was a year or two younger than he was. This boy tried to get Rafa to sit down but Rafa shook his head with that not-a-chance grin of his and before there could be an argument the driver shifted into gear, blasting the radio. *La chica de la novela* was still on the charts. Can you believe that? the man next to me said. They play that vaina a hundred times a day.

I lowered myself stiffly into my seat but the pastelito had already put a grease stain on my pants. Coño, I said and took out the pastelito and finished it in four bites. Rafa wasn't watching. Each time the autobus stopped he was hopping down and helping people bring on their packages. When a row filled he lowered the swing-down center seat for whoever was next. The cobrador, a thin boy with an Afro, was trying to keep up with him and the driver was too busy with his radio to notice what was happening. Two people paid Rafa – all of which Rafa gave to the cobrador, who was himself busy making change.

You have to watch out for stains like that, the man next to me said. He had big teeth and wore a clean fedora. His arms were ropy with muscles.

These things are too greasy, I said.

Let me help. He spit in his fingers and started to rub at the stain but then he was pinching at the tip of my pinga through the fabric of my shorts. He was smiling. I shoved him against his seat. He looked to see if anybody had noticed.

You pato, I said.

The man kept smiling.

You low-down pinga-sucking pato, I said. The man squeezed my bicep, quietly, hard, the way my friends would sneak me in church. I whimpered.

You should watch your mouth, he said.

I got up and went over to the door. Rafa slapped the roof and as the driver slowed the cobrador said, You two haven't paid.

Sure we did, Rafa said, pushing me down into the dusty street. I gave you the money for those two people there and I gave you our fare too. His voice was tired, as if he got into these discussions all the time.

No you didn't.

Fuck you I did. You got the fares. Why don't you count and see?

Don't even try it. The cobrador put his hand on Rafa but Rafa wasn't having it. He yelled up to the driver, Tell your boy to learn how to count.

We crossed the road and went down into a field of guineo; the cobrador was shouting after us and we stayed in the field until we heard the driver say, Forget them.

Rafa took off his shirt and fanned himself and that's when I started to cry.

He watched for a moment. You, he said, are a pussy.

I'm sorry.

What the hell's the matter with you? We didn't do anything wrong.

I'll be OK in a second. I sawed my forearm across my nose.

He took a look around, drawing in the lay of the land. If you can't stop crying, I'll leave you. He headed towards a shack that was rusting in the sun.

I watched him disappear. From the shack you could hear voices, as bright as chrome. Columns of ants had found a pile of meatless chicken bones at my feet and were industriously carting away the crumbling marrow. I could have gone home, which was what I usually did when Rafa acted up, but we were far – eight, nine miles away.

I caught up with him beyond the shack. We walked about a mile; my head felt cold and hollow.

Are you done?

Yes, I said.

Are you always going to be a pussy?

I wouldn't have raised my head if God himself had appeared in the sky and pissed down on us.

Rafa spit. You have to get tougher. Crying all the time. Do you think our papi's crying? Do you think that's what he's been doing the last six years? He turned from me. His feet were crackling through the weeds, breaking stems.

Rafa stopped a schoolboy in a blue and tan uniform, who pointed us down a road. Rafa spoke to a young mother, whose baby was hacking like a miner. A little further, she said and when he smiled she looked the other way. We went too far and a farmer with a machete showed us the easiest loop back. Rafa stopped when he saw Ysrael standing in the center of a field; he was flying a kite and despite the string he seemed almost unconnected to the distant wedge of black that finned back and forth in the sky. Here we go, Rafa said. I was embarrassed. What the hell were we supposed to do?

10

Stay close, he said. And get ready to run. He passed me his knife, then trotted down towards the field.

4

The summer before I pegged Ysrael with a rock and the way it bounced off his back I knew I'd clocked a shoulder blade.

You did it! You fucking did it! the other boys yelled.

He'd been running from us and he arched in pain and one of the other boys nearly caught him but he recovered and took off. He's faster than a mongoose, someone said, but in truth he was even faster than that. We laughed and went back to our baseball games and forgot him until he came to town again and then we dropped what we were doing and chased him. Show us your face, we cried. Let's see it just once.

5

He was about a foot bigger than either of us and looked like he'd been fattened on that supergrain the farmers around Ocoa were giving their stock, a new product which kept my tío up at night, muttering jealously, Proxyl Feed 9, Proxyl Feed 9. Ysrael's sandals were of stiff leather and his clothes were North American. I looked over at Rafa but my brother seemed unperturbed.

Listen up, Rafa said. My hermanito's not feeling too well. Can you show us where a colmado is? I want to get him a drink.

There's a faucet up the road, Ysrael said. His voice was odd and full of spit. His mask was handsewn from thin blue cotton fabric and you couldn't help but see the scar tissue that circled his left eye, a red waxy crescent, and the saliva that trickled down his neck.

We're not from around here. We can't drink the water.

Ysrael spooled in his string. The kite wheeled but he righted it with a yank.

Not bad, I said.

We can't drink the water around here. It would kill us. And he's already sick.

I smiled and tried to act sick, which wasn't too difficult. I was covered with dust and I saw Ysrael looking us over.

The water here is probably better than up in the mountains, he said.

Help us out, Rafa said in a low voice.

Ysrael pointed down a path. Just go that way, you'll find it.

Are you sure?

I've lived here all my life.

I could hear the plastic kite flapping in the wind; the string was coming in fast. Rafa huffed and started on his way. We made a long circle and by then Ysrael had his kite in hand – the kite was no handmade local job. It had been manufactured abroad.

We couldn't find it, Rafa said.

How stupid are you?

Where did you get that? I asked.

Nueva York, he said. From my father.

No shit! Our father's there too! I shouted.

I looked at Rafa, who, for an instant, frowned. Our father only sent us letters and an occasional shirt or pair of jeans at Christmas.

What the hell are you wearing that mask for anyway? Rafa asked.

I'm sick, Ysrael said.

It must be real hot.

Not for me.

Don't you take it off?

Not until I get better. I'm going to have an operation soon.

You better watch out for that, Rafa said. Those doctors will kill you faster than the guardia.

These are American doctors.

Rafa sniggered. You're lying.

I saw them last spring. They want me to go next year.

They're lying to you. They probably just felt sorry.

Do you want me to show you where the colmado is or not?

Sure.

Follow me, he said, wiping the spit on his neck. At the colmado he stood off while Rafa bought me the Cola. The owner was playing dominos with the beer delivery man and didn't bother to look up, though he put a hand in the air for Ysrael. He had that lean look of every colmado owner I'd ever met. On the way back to the road I left the bottle with Rafa to finish and caught up with Ysrael, who was ahead of us. Are you still into wrestling? I asked.

He turned to me and something rippled under the mask. How did you know that?

I heard, I said. Do they have wrestling in the States?

I hope so.

Are you a wrestler?

I'm a great wrestler. I almost went to fight in the Capital.

My brother laughed, swigging on the bottle.

You want to try it, pendejo?

Not right now.

I didn't think so.

13

I tapped his arm. The planes haven't dropped anything this year.

It's still too early. The first Sunday of August is when it starts.

How do you know?

I'm from around here, he said. The mask twitched. I realized he was smiling and then my brother brought his arm around and smashed the bottle on top of his head. It exploded, the thick bottom spinning away like a crazed eyeglass and I said, Holy fucking shit. Ysrael stumbled once and slammed into a fence post that had been sunk into the side of the road. Glass crumbled off his mask. He spun towards me, then fell down on his stomach. Rafa kicked him in the side. Ysrael seemed not to notice. He had his hands flat in the dirt and was concentrating on pushing himself up. Roll him on his back, my brother said and we did, pushing like crazy. Rafa took off his mask and threw it spinning into the grass.

His left ear was a nub and you could see the thick veined slab of his tongue through a hole in his cheek. He had no lips. His head was tipped back and his eyes had gone white and the cords were out on his neck. He'd been an infant when the pig had come into the house. The damage looked old but I still jumped back and said, Rafa, let's go! Rafa crouched and using only two of his fingers, turned Ysrael's head from side to side.

6

We went back to the colmado where the owner and the delivery man were now arguing, the dominos chattering under their hands. We kept walking and after one hour,

14

maybe two, we saw an autobus. We boarded and went right to the back. Rafa crossed his arms and watched the fields and roadside shacks scroll past, the dust and smoke and people almost frozen by our speed.

Ysrael will be OK, I said.

Don't bet on it.

They're going to fix him.

A muscle fluttered between his jaw bone and his ear. Yunior, he said tiredly. They aren't going to do shit to him.

How do you know?

I know, he said.

I put my feet on the back of the chair in front of me, pushing on an old lady, who looked back at me. She was wearing a baseball cap and one of her eyes was milky. The autobus was heading for Ocoa, not for home.

Rafa signaled for a stop. Get ready to run, he whispered.

I said, OK.

Fiesta 1980

Mami's youngest sister – my tía Yrma – finally made it to the
United States that year. She and tío Miguel got themselves
an apartment in the Bronx, off the Grand Concourse, and
everybody decided that we should have a party. Actually,
my pops decided, but everybody – meaning Mami, tía
Yrma, tío Miguel, and their neighbors – thought it a dope
idea. On the afternoon of the party Papi came back from
work around six. Right on time. We were all dressed by
then, which was a smart move on our part. If Papi had
walked in and caught us lounging around in our underwear, he would have kicked our asses something serious.

He didn't say nothing to nobody, not even my moms.
He just pushed past her, held up his hand when she tried
to talk to him and headed right into the shower. Rafa gave
me the look and I gave it back to him; we both knew Papi
had been with that Puerto Rican woman he was seeing and
wanted to wash off the evidence quick.

Mami looked really nice that day. The United States had
finally put some meat on her; she was no longer the same
flaca who had arrived here three years before. She had cut
her hair short and was wearing tons of cheap-ass jewelry
which on her didn't look too lousy. She smelled like herself, like the wind through a tree. She always waited until

the last possible minute to put on her perfume because she said it was a waste to spray it on early and then have to spray it on again once you got to the party.

We – meaning me, my brother, my little sister and Mami – waited for Papi to finish his shower. Mami seemed anxious, in her usual dispassionate way. Her hands adjusted the buckle of her belt over and over again. That morning, when she had gotten us up for school, Mami told us that she wanted to have a good time at the party. I want to dance, she said, but now, with the sun sliding out of the sky like spit off a wall, she seemed ready to just get this over with.

Rafa didn't much want to go to no party either, and me, I never wanted to go anywhere with my family. There was a baseball game in the parking lot outside and we could hear our friends, yelling Hey and You suck to one another. We heard the pop of a ball as it sailed over the cars, the clatter of an aluminum bat dropping to the concrete. Not that me or Rafa loved baseball; we just liked playing with the local kids, thrashing them at anything they were doing. By the sounds of the shouting, we both knew the game was close, either of us could have made a difference. Rafa frowned and when I frowned back, he put up his fist. Don't you mirror me, he said.

Don't you mirror me, I said.

He punched me – I would have hit him back but Papi marched into the living room with his towel around his waist, looking a lot smaller than he did when he was dressed. He had a few strands of hair around his nipples and a surly closed-mouth expression, like maybe he'd scalded his tongue or something.

Have they eaten? he asked Mami.

She nodded. I made you something.

You didn't let him eat, did you?

Ay, Dios mio, she said, letting her arms fall to her side.

Ay, Dios mio is right, Papi said.

I was never supposed to eat before our car trips, but earlier, when she had put out our dinner of rice, beans and sweet platanos, guess who had been the first one to clean his plate? You couldn't blame Mami really, she had been busy – cooking, getting ready, dressing my sister Madai. I should have reminded her not to feed me but I wasn't that sort of son.

Papi turned to me. Coño, muchacho, why did you eat?

Rafa had already started inching away from me. I'd once told him I considered him a low-down chicken-shit for moving out of the way every time Papi was going to smack me.

Collateral damage, Rafa had said. Ever heard of it?

No.

Look it up.

Chicken-shit or not, I didn't dare glance at him. Papi was old-fashioned; he expected your undivided attention when you were getting your ass whupped. You couldn't look him in the eye either – that wasn't allowed. Better to stare at his belly button which was round and immaculate. Papi pulled me to my feet by my ear.

If you throw up –

I won't, I cried, tears in my eyes, more out of reflex than pain.

Ya, Ramón, ya. It's not his fault, Mami said.

They've known about this party forever. How did they

19

think we were going to get there? Fly?

He finally let go of my ear and I sat back down. Madai was too scared to open her eyes. Being around Papi all her life had turned her into a major-league wuss. Anytime Papi raised his voice her lip would start trembling, like some specialized tuning fork. Rafa pretended that he had knuckles to crack, and when I shoved him he gave me a *Don't start* look. But even that little bit of recognition made me feel better.

I was the one who was always in trouble with my dad. It was like my God-given duty to piss him off, to do everything the way he hated. Our fights didn't bother me too much. I still wanted him to love me, something that never seemed strange or contradictory until years later, when he was out of our lives.

By the time my ear stopped stinging Papi was dressed and Mami was crossing each one of us, solemnly, like we were heading off to war. We said, in turn, Bendición, Mami, and she poked us in our five cardinal spots while saying, Que Dios te bendiga.

This was how all our trips began, the words that followed me every time I left the house.

None of us spoke until we were inside Papi's Volkswagen van. Brand new, lime-green and bought to impress. Oh, we were impressed, but me, every time I was in that VW and Papi went above twenty miles an hour, I vomited. I'd never had trouble with cars before – that van was like my curse. Mami suspected it was the upholstery. In her mind, American things – appliances, mouth wash, funny-looking upholstery – all seemed to have an intrinsic badness about them. Papi was careful about taking me anywhere in the VW, but when he had to, I rode up front in Mami's usual seat so I could throw up out a window.

¿Cómo te sientes? Mami asked over my shoulder when Papi pulled onto the Turnpike. She had her hand on the base of my neck. One thing about Mami, her palms never sweated.

I'm OK, I said, keeping my eyes straight ahead. I definitely didn't want to trade glances with Papi. He had this one look, furious and sharp, that always left me feeling bruised.

Toma. Mami handed me four mentas. She had thrown three out her window at the beginning of our trip, an offering to Eshú; the rest were for me.

I took one and sucked it slowly, my tongue knocking it up against my teeth. We passed Newark Airport without any incident. If Madai had been awake she would have cried because the planes flew so close to the cars.

How's he feeling? Papi asked.

Fine, I said. I glanced back at Rafa and he pretended like he didn't see me. That was the way he was, at school and at home. When I was in trouble, he didn't know me. Madai was solidly asleep, but even with her face all wrinkled-up and drooling she looked cute, her hair all separated into patches.

I turned around and concentrated on the candy. Papi even started to joke that we might not have to scrub the van out tonight. He was beginning to loosen up, not checking at his watch too much. Maybe he was thinking about that Puerto Rican woman or maybe he was just happy that we were all together. I could never tell. At the toll, he was feeling positive enough to actually get out of the van and search around under the basket for dropped coins. It was something he had once done to amuse Madai, but now it was habit. Cars behind us honked their horns and I slid down in my seat. Rafa didn't care; he grinned back at the other cars and waved. His actual job was to make sure no cops were coming. Mami shook Madai awake and as soon as she saw Papi stooping for a couple of quarters she let out this screech of delight that almost took off the top of my head.

That was the end of the good times. Just outside the Washington Bridge, I started feeling woozy. The smell of the upholstery got all up inside my head and I found myself with a mouthful of saliva. Mami's hand tensed on my shoulder and when I caught Papi's eye, he was like, No way. Don't do it.

The first time I got sick in the van Papi was taking me to the library. Rafa was with us and he couldn't believe I threw up. I was famous for my steel-lined stomach. A third-world childhood could give you that. Papi was worried enough that just as quick as Rafa could drop off the books we were on our way home. Mami fixed me one of her honey-and-onion concoctions and that made my stomach feel better. A week later we tried the library again and on this go-around I couldn't get the window open in time. When Papi got me home, he went and cleaned out the van himself, an expression of askho on his face. This was a big deal, since Papi almost never cleaned anything himself. He came back inside and found me sitting on the couch feeling like hell.

It's the car, he said to Mami. It's making him sick.

This time the damage was pretty minimal, nothing Papi couldn't wash off the door with a blast of the hose. He was pissed, though; he jammed his finger into my cheek, a nice solid thrust. That was the way he was with his punishments: imaginative. Earlier that year I'd written an essay in school called MY FATHER THE TORTURER, but the teacher made me write a new one. She thought I was kidding.

We drove the rest of the way to the Bronx in silence. We only stopped once, so I could brush my teeth. Mami had brought along my toothbrush and a tube of toothpaste and while every car known to man sped by us she stood outside with me so I wouldn't feel alone.

Tío Miguel was about seven feet tall and had his hair combed up and out, into a demi-fro. He gave me and Rafa big spleen-crushing hugs and then kissed Mami and finally ended up with Madai on his shoulder. The last time I'd seen Tío was at the airport, his first day in the United States. I remembered how he hadn't seemed all that troubled to be in another country.

He looked down at me. Carajo, Yunior, you look horrible!

He threw up, my brother explained.

I pushed Rafa. Thanks a lot, ass-face.

Hey, he said. Tío asked.

Tío clapped a bricklayer's hand on my shoulder. Everybody gets sick sometimes, he said. You should have seen me on the plane over here. Dios mio! He rolled his Asian-looking eyes for emphasis. I thought we were all going to die.

Everybody could tell he was lying. I smiled like he was making me feel better.

Do you want me to get you a drink? Tío asked. We got beer and rum.

23

Miguel, Mami said. He's young.

Young? Back in Santo Domingo, he'd be getting laid by now.

Mami thinned her lips, which took some doing.

Well, it's true, Tío said.

So, Mami, I said. When do I get to go visit the DR?

That's enough, Yunior.

It's the only pussy you'll ever get, Rafa said to me in English.

Not counting your girlfriend, of course.

Rafa smiled. He had to give me that one.

Papi came in from parking the van. He and Miguel gave each other the sort of handshakes that would have turned my fingers into Wonderbread.

Coño, compa'i, ¿cómo va todo? they said to each other.

Tía came out then, with an apron on and maybe the longest Lee-Press-On nails I've ever seen in my life. There was this one guru motherfucker in the *Guinness Book of World Records* who had longer nails, but I tell you, it was close. She gave everybody kisses, told me and Rafa how guapo we were – Rafa, of course, believed her – told Madai how bella she was, but when she got to Papi, she froze a little, like maybe she'd seen a wasp on the tip of his nose, but then kissed him all the same.

Mami told us to join the other kids in the living room. Tío said, Wait a minute, I want to show you the apartment. I was glad Tía said Hold on, because from what I'd seen so far, the place had been furnished in Contemporary Dominican Tacky. The less I saw, the better. I mean, I liked plastic sofa covers but damn, Tío and Tía had taken it to another level. They had a disco ball hanging in the living

room and the type of stucco ceilings that looked like sta-
lactite heaven. The sofas all had golden tassels dangling
from their edges. Tía came out of the kitchen with some
people I didn't know and by the time she got done intro-
ducing everybody, only Papi and Mami were given the
guided tour of the four-room third-floor apartment. Me
and Rafa joined the kids in the living room. They'd already
started eating. We were hungry, one of the girls explained,
a pastelito in hand. The boy was about three years younger
than me but the girl who'd spoken, Leti, was my age. She
and another girl were on the sofa together and they were
cute as hell.

Leti introduced them: the boy was her brother Wilquins
and the other girl was her neighbor Mari. Leti had some serious tetas and I could tell that my brother was going to gun
for her. His taste in girls was predictable. He sat down right
between Leti and Mari and by the way they were smiling at
him I knew he'd do fine. Neither of the girls gave me more
than a cursory one-two, which didn't bother me. Sure, I liked
girls but I was always too terrified to speak to them unless
we were arguing or I was calling them stupidos, which was
one of my favorite words that year. I turned to Wilquins and
asked him what there was to do around here. Mari, who had
the lowest voice I'd ever heard, said, He can't speak.

What does that mean?

He's mute.

I looked at Wilquins incredulously. He smiled and nodded, as if he'd won a prize or something.

Does he understand? I asked.

Of course he understands, Rafa said. He's not dumb.

I could tell Rafa had said that just to score points with

the girls. Both of them nodded. Low-voice Mari said, He's the best student in his grade.

I thought, Not bad for a mute. I sat next to Wilquins. After about two seconds of TV Wilquins whipped out a bag of dominos and motioned to me. Did I want to play? Sure. Me and him played Rafa and Leti and we whupped their collective asses twice, which put Rafa in a real bad mood. He looked at me like maybe he wanted to take a swing, just one to make him feel better. Leti kept whispering into Rafa's ear, telling him it was OK.

In the kitchen I could hear my parents slipping into their usual modes. Papi's voice was loud and argumentative; you didn't have to be anywhere near him to catch his drift. And Mami, you had to put cups to your ears to hear hers. I went into the kitchen a few times – once so the tíos could show off how much bullshit I'd been able to cram in my head the last few years; another time for a bucket-sized cup of soda. Mami and Tía were frying tostones and the last of the pastelitos. Mami appeared happier now and the way her hands worked on our dinner you would think she had a life somewhere else making rare and precious things. She nudged Tía every now and then, shit they must have been doing it all their lives. As soon as Mami saw me though, she gave me the eye. Don't stay long, that eye said. Don't piss your old man off.

Papi was too busy arguing about Elvis to notice me. Then somebody mentioned María Montez and Papi barked, María Montez? Let me tell you about María Montez, compa'i.

Maybe I was used to him. His voice – louder than most adults – didn't bother me none, though the other kids shifted uneasily in their seats. Wilquins was about to raise the volume on the TV, but Rafa said, I wouldn't do that. Muteboy had balls, though. He did it anyway and then sat down. Wilquins's pop came into the living room a second later, a bottle of Presidente in hand. That dude must have had Spider-senses or something. Did you raise that? he asked Wilquins and Wilquins nodded.

Is this your house? his pops asked. He looked ready to beat Wilquins silly but he lowered the volume instead.

See, Rafa said. You nearly got your ass *kicked*.

I met the Puerto Rican woman right after Papi had gotten the van. He was taking me on short trips, trying to cure me of my vomiting. It wasn't really working but I looked forward to our trips, even though at the end of each one I'd be sick. These were the only times me and Papi did anything together. When we were alone he treated me much better, like maybe I was his son or something.

Before each drive Mami would cross me.

Bendición, Mami, I'd say.

She'd kiss my forehead. Que Dios te bendiga. And then she would give me a handful of mentas because she wanted me to be OK. Mami didn't think these excursions would cure anything, but the one time she had brought it up to Papi he had told her to shut up, what did she know about anything anyway?

Me and Papi didn't talk much. We just drove around our neighborhood. Occasionally he'd ask, How is it?

And I'd nod, no matter how I felt.

One day I was sick outside of Perth Amboy. Instead of taking me home he went the other way on Industrial Avenue, stopping a few minutes later in front of a light-blue house I didn't recognize. It reminded me of the Easter eggs we colored at school, the ones we threw out the bus windows at other cars.

The Puerto Rican woman was there and she helped me clean up. She had dry papery hands and when she rubbed the towel on my chest, she did it hard, like I was a bumper she was waxing. She was very thin and had a cloud of brown hair rising above her narrow face and the sharpest blackest eyes you've ever seen.

He's cute, she said to Papi.

Not when he's throwing up, Papi said.

What's your name? she asked me. Are you Rafa?

I shook my head.

Then it's Yunior, right?

I nodded.

You're the smart one, she said, suddenly happy with herself. Maybe you want to see my books?

They weren't hers. I recognized them as ones my father must have left in her house. Papi was a voracious reader, couldn't even go cheating without a paperback in his pocket.

Why don't you go watch TV? Papi suggested. He was looking at her like she was the last piece of chicken on earth.

We got plenty of channels, she said. Use the remote if you want.

The two of them went upstairs and I was too scared of what was happening to poke around. I just sat there, ashamed, expecting something big and fiery to crash down on our heads. I watched a whole hour of the news before Papi came downstairs and said, Let's go.

About two hours later the women laid out the food and

like always nobody but the kids thanked them. It must be some Dominican tradition or something. There was everything I liked – chicharrónes, fried chicken, tostones, sancocho, rice, fried cheese, yuca, avocado, potato salad, a meteor-sized hunk of pernil, even a tossed salad which I could do without – but when I joined the other kids around the serving table, Papi said, Oh no, you don't, and took the paper plate out of my hand. His fingers weren't gentle.

What's wrong now? Tía asked, handing me another plate.

He ain't eating, Papi said. Mami pretended to help Rafa with the pernil.

Why can't he eat?

Because I said so.

The adults who didn't know us made like they hadn't heard a thing and Tío just smiled sheepishly and told everybody to go ahead and eat. All the kids – about ten of them now – trooped back into the living room with their plates a-heaping and all the adults ducked into the kitchen and the dining room, where the radio was playing loud-ass bachatas. I was the only one without a plate. Papi stopped me before I could get away from him. He kept his voice nice and low so nobody else could hear him.

If you eat anything, I'm going to beat you. ¿Entiendes?

I nodded.

And if your brother gives you any food, I'll beat him too. Right here in front of everybody. ¿Entiendes?

I nodded again. I wanted to kill him and he must have sensed it because he gave my head a little shove.

All the kids watched me come in and sit down in front of the TV.

29

What's wrong with your dad? Leti asked.

He's a dick, I said.

Rafa shook his head. Don't say that shit in front of people.

Easy for you to be nice when you're eating, I said.

Hey, if I was a pukey little baby, I wouldn't get no food either.

I almost said something back but I concentrated on the TV. I wasn't going to start it. No fucking way. So I watched Bruce Lee beat Chuck Norris into the floor of the Coliseum and tried to pretend that there was no food anywhere in the house. It was Tía who finally saved me. She came into the living room and said, Since you ain't eating, Yunior, you can at least help me get some ice.

I didn't want to, but she mistook my reluctance for something else.

I already asked your father.

She held my hand while we walked; Tía didn't have any kids but I could tell she wanted them. She was the sort of relative who always remembered your birthday but who you only went to visit because you had to. We didn't get past the first-floor landing before she opened her pocket-book and handed me the first of three pastelitos she had smuggled out of the apartment.

Go ahead, she said. And as soon as you get inside make sure you brush your teeth.

Thanks a lot, Tía, I said.

Those pastelitos didn't stand a chance.

She sat next to me on the stairs and smoked her ciga-rette. All the way down on the first floor and we could still hear the music and the adults and the television. Tía looked a ton like Mami; the two of them were both short

30

and light-skinned. Tía smiled a lot and that was what set them apart the most.

How is it at home, Yunior?

What do you mean?

How's it going in the apartment? Are you kids OK?

I knew an interrogation when I heard one, no matter how sugar-coated it was. I didn't say anything. Don't get me wrong, I loved my tía, but something told me to keep my mouth shut. Maybe it was family loyalty, maybe I just wanted to protect Mami or I was afraid that Papi would find out – it could have been anything really.

Is your mom all right?

I shrugged.

Have there been lots of fights?

None, I said. Too many shrugs would have been just as bad as an answer. Papi's at work too much.

Work, Tía said, like it was somebody's name she didn't like.

Me and Rafa, we didn't talk much about the Puerto Rican woman. When we ate dinner at her house, the few times Papi had taken us over there, we still acted like nothing was out of the ordinary. Pass the ketchup, man. No sweat, bro. The affair was like a hole in our living room floor, one we'd gotten so used to circumnavigating that we sometimes forgot it was there.

By midnight all the adults were crazy dancing. I was sitting outside Tía's bedroom, where Madai was sleeping, trying not to attract attention. Rafa had me guarding the door; he and Leti were in there too, with some of the other

31

kids, getting busy no doubt. Wilquins had gone across the hall to bed so I had me and the roaches to mess around with.

Whenever I peered into the main room I saw about twenty moms and dads dancing and drinking beers. Every now and then somebody yelled, Quisqueya! And then everybody else would yell and stomp their feet. From what I could see my parents seemed to be enjoying themselves.

Mami and Tía spent a lot of time side by side, whispering, and I kept expecting something to come of this, a brawl maybe. I'd never once been out with my family when it hadn't turned to shit. We weren't even theatrical or straight crazy like other families. We fought like sixth-graders, without any real dignity. I guess the whole night I'd been waiting for a blow-up, something between Papi and Mami. This was how I always figured Papi would be exposed, out in public, where everybody would know.

You're a cheater!

But everything was calmer than usual. And Mami didn't look like she was about to say anything to Papi. The two of them danced every now and then but they never lasted more than a song before Mami joined Tía again in whatever conversation they were having.

I tried to imagine Mami before Papi. Maybe I was tired, or just sad, thinking about the way my family was. Maybe I already knew how it would all end up in a few years, Mami without Papi, and that was why I did it. Picturing her alone wasn't easy. It seemed like Papi had always been with her, even when we were waiting in Santo Domingo for him to send for us.

The only photograph our family had of Mami as a young woman, before she married Papi, was the one that somebody took of her at an election party that I found one day while rummaging for money to go to the arcade. Mami had it tucked into her immigration papers. In the photo, she's surrounded by laughing cousins I will never meet, who are all shiny from dancing, whose clothes are rumpled and loose. You can tell it's night and hot and that the mosquitos have been biting. She sits straight and even in a crowd she stands out, smiling quietly like maybe she's the one everybody's celebrating. You can't see her hands but I imagined they're knotting a straw or a bit of thread. This was the woman my father met a year later on the Malecón, the woman Mami thought she'd always be.

Mami must have caught me studying her because she stopped what she was doing and gave me a smile, maybe her first one of the night. Suddenly I wanted to go over and hug her, for no other reason than I loved her, but there were about eleven fat jiggling bodies between us. So I sat down on the tiled floor and waited.

I must have fallen asleep because the next thing I knew Rafa was kicking me and saying, Let's go. He looked like he'd been hitting those girls off; he was all smiles. I got to my feet in time to kiss Tía and Tío good-bye. Mami was holding the serving dish she had brought with her.

Where's Papi? I asked.

He's downstairs, bringing the van around. Mami leaned down to kiss me.

You were good today, she said.

And then Papi burst in and told us to get the hell downstairs before some pendejo cop gave him a ticket. More kisses, more handshakes and then we were gone.

33

I don't remember being out-of-sorts after I met the Puerto Rican woman, but I must have been because Mami only asked me questions when she thought something was wrong in my life. It took her about ten passes but finally she cornered me one afternoon when we were alone in the apartment. Our upstairs neighbors were beating the crap out of their kids, and me and her had been listening to it all afternoon. She put her hand on mine and said, Is everything OK, Yunior? Have you been fighting with your brother?

Me and Rafa had already talked. We'd been in the basement, where our parents couldn't hear us. He told me that yeah, he knew about her.

Papi's taken me there twice now.

Why didn't you tell me? I asked

What the hell was I going to say? *Hey, Yunior, guess what happened yesterday? I met Papi's sucia!*

I didn't say anything to Mami either. She watched me, very very closely. Later I would think, maybe if I had told her, she would have confronted him, would have done something, but who can know these things? I said I'd been having trouble in school and like that everything was back to normal between us. She put her hand on my shoulder and squeezed and that was that.

We were on the Turnpike, just past Exit 11, when I started feeling it again. I sat up from leaning against Rafa. His fingers smelled and he'd gone to sleep almost as soon as he got into the van. Madai was out too but at least she wasn't snoring.

In the darkness, I saw that Papi had a hand on Mami's knee and that the two of them were quiet and still. They weren't slumped back or anything; they were both wide awake, bolted into their seats. I couldn't see either of their faces and no matter how hard I tried I could not imagine their expressions. Neither of them moved. Every now and then the van was filled with the bright rush of somebody else's headlights. Finally I said, Mami, and they both looked back, already knowing what was happening.

Aurora

Earlier today me and Cut drove down to South River and bought us some more smoke. The regular pick-up, enough to last us the rest of the month. The Peruvian dude who hooks us up gave us a sampler of his superweed (jewel luv it, he said) and on the way home, past the Hydrox factory, we could have sworn we smelled cookies baking right in the back seat. Cut was smelling chocolate chip but I was smoothed out on those rocky coconut ones we used to get at school.

Holy shit, Cut said. I'm drooling all over myself.

I looked over at him but the black stubble on his chin and neck was dry. This shit is potent, I said.

That's the word I'm looking for. Potent.

Strong, I said.

It took us four hours of TV to sort, weigh and bag the smoke. We were puffing the whole way through and by the time we were in bed we were gone. Cut's still giggling over the cookies and me, I'm just waiting for Aurora to show up. Fridays are good days to expect her. Fridays are smoke days and she knows it.

We haven't seen each other for a week. Not since she put some scratches on my arm. Fading now, like you could rub them with spit and they'd go away but when she first

37

put them there, with her sharp-ass nails, they were long and swollen.

Around midnight I hear her tapping on the basement window. She calls my name maybe four times before I say, I'm going out to talk to her.

Don't do it, Cut says. Just leave it alone.

He's not a fan of Aurora, never gives me the messages she leaves with him. I've found these notes in his pockets and under our couches. Bullshit mostly but every now and then she leaves one that makes me want to treat her better. I lie in bed some more, listening to our neighbors flush parts of themselves down a pipe. She stops tapping, maybe to smoke a cigarette or just to listen for my breathing.

Cut rolls over. Leave it bro.

I'm going, I say.

She meets me at the door of the utility room, a single bulb lit behind her. I shut the door behind us and we kiss, once, on the lips, but she keeps them closed, first-date style. A few months ago Cut broke the lock to this place and now the utility room's ours, like an extension, an office. Concrete with splotches of oil. A drain hole in the corner where we throw our cigs and condoms.

She's skinny – six months out of juvie and she's skinny like a twelve-year-old.

I want some company, she says.

Where are the dogs?

You know they don't like you. She looks out the window, all tagged over with initials and fuck yous. It's going to rain, she says.

It always looks like that.

Yeah, but this time it's going to rain for real.

I put my ass down on the old mattress, which stinks of pussy.

Where's your partner? she asks.

He's sleeping.

That's all that nigger does. She's got the shakes – even in this light I can see that. Hard to kiss anyone like that, hard even to touch them – the flesh moves like it's on rollers. She yanks open the drawstrings on her knapsack and pulls out cigarettes. She's living out of her bag again, on cigarettes and dirty clothes. I see a T-shirt, a couple of tampons and those same green shorts, the thin high-cut ones I bought her last summer.

Where you been? I ask. Haven't seen you around.

You know me. Yo ando más que un perro.

Her hair is dark with water. She must have gotten herself a shower, maybe at a friend's, maybe in an empty apartment. I know that I should dis her for being away so long, that Cut's probably listening, but I take her hand and kiss it.

Come on, I say.

You ain't said nothing about the last time.

I can't remember no last time. I just remember you.

She looks at me like maybe she's going to shove my smooth-ass line back down my throat. Then her face becomes smooth. Do you want to jig?

Yeah, I say. I push her back on that mattress and grab at her clothes. Go easy, she says.

I can't help myself with her and being blunted makes it worse. She has her hands on my shoulder blades and the way she pulls on them I think maybe she's trying to open me.

Go easy, she says.

We all do shit like this, stuff that's no good for you. You

do it and then there's no feeling positive about it afterward. When Cut puts his salsa on the next morning, I wake up, alone, the blood doing jumping jacks in my head. I see that she's searched my pockets, left them hanging out of my pants like tongues. She didn't even bother to push the fuckers back in.

A Working Day

Raining this morning. We hit the crowd at the bus stop, pass by the trailer park across Route 9, near the Audio Shack. Dropping rocks all over. Ten here, ten there, an ounce of weed for the big guy with the warts, some H for his coked-up girl, the one with the bloody left eye. Everybody's buying for the holiday weekend. Each time I put a bag in a hand I say, Pow, right there, my man.

Cut says he heard us last night, rides me the whole time about it. I'm surprised the AIDS ain't bit your dick off yet, he says.

I'm immune, I tell him. He looks at me and tells me to keep talking. Just keep talking, he says.

Four calls come in and we take the Pathfinder out to South Amboy and Freehold. Then it's back to the Terrace for more foot action. That's the way we run things, the less driving, the better.

None of our customers are anybody special. We don't have priests or abuelas or police officers on our lists. Just a lot of kids and some older folks who haven't had a job or a haircut since the last census. I have friends in Perth Amboy and New Brunswick who tell me they deal to whole families, from the grandparents down to the fourth graders. Things around here aren't like that yet, but more kids are dealing and bigger crews are coming in from out of town, relatives of folks who live here. We're still making mad paper but it's harder now and Cut's already been sliced once and me, I'm thinking it's time to grow, to incorporate but Cut says, Fuck no. The smaller the better.

We're reliable and easy-going and that keeps us good with the older people, who don't want shit from anybody. Me, I'm tight with the kids, that's my side of the business. We work all hours of the day and when Cut goes to see his girl I keep at it, prowling up and down Westminister, saying wassup to everybody. I'm good for solo work. I'm edgy and don't like to be inside too much. You should have seen me in school. Olvidate.

One of Our Nights

We hurt each other too well to let it drop. She breaks everything I own, yells at me like it might change something, tries to slam doors on my fingers. When she wants me to promise her a love that's never been seen anywhere I think about the other girls. The last one was on Kean's women's basketball team, with skin that made mine look dark. A college girl with her own car, who came over right after her games, in her uniform, mad at some other school for a bad lay-up or an elbow in the chin.

Tonight me and Aurora sit in front of the TV and split a case of Budweiser. This is going to hurt, she says, holding her can up. There's H too, a little for her, a little for me. Upstairs my neighbors have their own long night going and they're laying out all their cards about one another. Big cruel loud cards.

Listen to that romance, she says.

It's all sweet talk, I say. They're yelling because they're in love.

She picks off my glasses and kisses the parts of my face that almost never get touched, the skin under the glass and frame.

You got those long eyelashes that make me want to cry, she says. How could anybody hurt a man with eyelashes like this?

I don't know, I say, though she should. She once tried to jam a pen in my thigh, but that was the night I punched her chest black and blue so I don't think it counts.

I pass out first, like always. I catch flashes from the movie before I'm completely gone. A man pouring too much Scotch into a plastic cup. A couple running toward each other. I wish I could stay awake through a thousand bad shows the way she does, but it's OK as long as she's breathing past the side of my neck.

Later I open my eyes and catch her kissing Cut. She's pumping her hips into him and he's got his hairy-ass hands in her hair. Fuck, I say but then I wake up and she's snoring on the couch. I put my hand on her side. She's barely nineteen, too skinny for anybody but me. She has her pipe right on the table, waited for me to fall out before hitting it. I have to open the porch door to kill the smell. I go back to sleep and when I wake up in the morning I'm laying in the tub and I've got blood on my chin and I can't remember how in the world that happened. This is no good, I tell myself. I go into the sala, wanting her to be there but she's gone again and I punch myself in the nose just to clear my head.

Love

We don't see each other much. Twice a month, four times maybe. Time don't flow right with me these days but I know it ain't often. I got my own life now, she tells me but you don't need to be an expert to see that she's flying again. That's what she's got going on, that's what's new.

We were tighter before she got sent to juvie, much tighter. Every day we chilled and if we needed a place we'd find ourselves an empty apartment, one that hadn't been rented yet. We'd break in. Smash a window, slide it up, wiggle on through. We'd bring sheets, pillows, and candles to make the place less cold. Aurora would color the walls, draw different pictures with crayons, splatter the red wax from the candles into patterns, beautiful patterns. You got talent, I told her and she laughed. I used to be real good at art. Real good. We'd have these apartments for a couple of weeks, until the supers came to clean for the next tenants and then we'd come by and find the window fixed and the lock on the door.

On some nights – especially when Cut's fucking his girl in the next bed – I want us to be like that again. I think I'm one of those guys who lives too much in the past. Cut'll be working his girl and she'll be like, Oh yes, dámelo duro, Papi, and I'll just get dressed and go looking for her ass. She still does the apartment thing but hangs out with a gang of crackheads, one of two girls there, sticks with this boy Harry. She says he's like her brother but I know better. Harry's a little pato, a cabrón, twice beat by Cut, twice beat by me. On the nights I find her she clings to him like she's his other nut, never wants to step outside for a minute. The others ask me if I have anything, giving me bullshit looks like they're hard or something. Do you have anything? Harry's moaning, his head caught between his knees like a big ripe coconut. Anything? I say No, and grab onto her bicep, lead her into the bedroom. She slumps against the closet door. I thought maybe you'd want to get something to eat, I say.

I ate. You got cigarettes?

I give her a fresh pack. She holds it lightly, debating if she should smoke a few or sell the pack to somebody.

I can give you another, I say and she asks why I have to be such an ass.

I'm just offering.

Don't offer me anything with that voice.

Just go easy, nena.

We smoke a couple, her hissing out smoke, and then I close the plastic blinds. Sometimes I have condoms but not every time and while she says she ain't with anybody else, I don't kid myself. Harry's yelling, What the fuck are you doing? but he doesn't touch the door, doesn't even knock. After, when she's picking at my back and the others in the next room have started talking again, I'm amazed at how nasty I feel, how I want to put my fist in her face.

I don't always find her; she spends a lot of time at the Hacienda, with the rest of her fucked-up friends. I find unlocked doors and Dorito crumbs, maybe an unflushed toilet. Always puke, in a closet or on a wall. Sometimes folks take craps right on the living room floor; I've learned not to walk around until my eyes get used to the dark. I go from room to room, hand out in front of me, wishing that maybe just this once I'll feel her soft face on the other side of my fingers instead of some fucking plaster wall. Once that actually happened, a long time ago.

The apartments are all the same, no surprises whatso-
ever. I wash my hands in the sink, dry them on the walls
and head out.

Corner

You watch anything long enough and you can become an
expert at it. Get to know how it lives, what it eats. Tonight
the corner is cold and nothing is really going on. You can
hear the dice clicking on the curb and every truck and
souped-up shitmobile that rolls in from the highway
announces itself with bass.

The corner's where you smoke, eat, fuck, where you play
selo. Selo games like you've never seen. I know brothers
who make two, three hundred a night on the dice. Always
somebody losing big. But you have to be careful with that.
Never know who'll lose and then come back with a 9 or a
machete, looking for the rematch. I follow Cut's advice and
do my dealing nice and tranquilo, no flash, not a lot of talking. I'm cool with everybody and when folks show up they
always give me a pound, knock their shoulder into mine,
ask me how it's been. Cut talks to his girl, pulling her long
hair, messing with her little boy but his eyes are always
watching the road for cops, like minesweepers.

We're all under the big street lamps, everyone's the
color of day-old piss. When I'm fifty this is how I'll remember my friends: tired and yellow and drunk. Eggie's out
here too. Homeboy's got himself an afro and his big head
looks ridiculous on his skinny-ass neck. He's way-out high
tonight. Back in the day, before Cut's girl took over, he was
Cut's gunboy but he was an irresponsible motherfucker,

45

showed it around too much and talked amazing amounts of shit. He's arguing with some of the tígueres over nonsense and when he doesn't back down I can see that nobody's happy. The corner's hot now and I just shake my head. Nelo, the nigger Eggie's talking shit to, has had more PTI than most of us have had traffic tickets. I ain't in the mood for this shit.

I ask Cut if he wants burgers and his girl's boy trots over and says, Get me two.

Come back quick, Cut says, all about business. He tries to hand me bills but I laugh, tell him it's on me.

The Pathfinder sits in the next parking lot, crusty with mud but still a slamming ride. I'm in no rush; I take it out behind the apartments, onto the road that leads to the dump. This was our spot when we were younger, where we started fires we sometimes couldn't keep down. Whole areas around the road are still black. Everything that catches in my headlights – the stack of old tires, signs, shacks – has a memory scratched onto it. Here's where I shot my first pistol. Here's where we stashed our porn magazines. Here's where I kissed my first girl.

I get to the restaurant late; the lights are out but I know the girl in the front and she lets me in. She's heavy but has a good face, makes me think of the one time we kissed, when I put my hand in her pants and felt the pad she had on. I ask her about her mother and she says, Regular. The brother? Still down in Virginia with the Navy. Don't let him turn into no pato. She laughs, pulls at the nameplate around her neck. Any woman who laughs as dope as she does won't ever have trouble finding men. I tell her that and she looks a little scared of me. She gives me what she has under the lamps for free and when I get back to the corner Eggie's out cold on the grass. A couple of older kids stand around him, pissing hard streams into his face. Come on, Eggie, somebody says. Open that mouth. Supper's coming. Cut's laughing too hard to talk to me and he ain't the only one. Brothers are falling over with laughter and some grab onto their boys, pretend to smash their heads against the curb. I give the boy his hamburgers and he goes between two bushes, where no one will bother him. He squats down and unfolds the oily paper, careful not to stain his Carhardt. Why don't you give me a piece of that? some girl asks him.

Because I'm hungry, he says, taking a big bite out.

Lucero

I would have named it after you, she said. She folded my shirt and put it on the kitchen counter. Nothing in the apartment, only us naked and some beer and half a pizza, cold and greasy. You're named after a star.

This was before I knew about the kid. She kept going on like that and finally I said, What the fuck are you talking about?

She picked the shirt up and folded it again, patting it down like this had taken her some serious effort. I'm telling you something. Something about me. What you should be doing is listening.

I Could Save You

I find her outside the Quick Check, hot with a fever. She wants to go to the Hacienda but not alone. Come on, she says, her palm on my shoulder.

Are you in trouble?

Fuck that. I just want company.

I know I should just go home. The cops bust the Hacienda about twice a year, like it's a holiday. Today could be my lucky day. Today could be our lucky day.

You don't have to come inside. Just hang with me a little.

If something inside of me is saying no, why do I say Yeah, sure?

We walk up to Route 9 and wait for the other side to clear. Cars buzz past and a new Pontiac swerves towards us, a scare, streetlights flowing back over its top, but we're too lifted to flinch. The driver's blond and laughing and we give him the finger. We watch the cars and above us the sky has gone the color of pumpkins. I haven't seen her in ten days, but she's steady, her hair combed back straight, like she was back in school or something. My mom's getting married, she says.

To that radiator guy?

No, some other guy. Owns a carwash.

That's real nice. She's lucky for her age.

You want to come with me to the wedding?

I put my cigarette out. Why can't I see us there? Her smoking in the bathroom and me dealing to the groom. I don't know about that.

My mom sent me money to buy a dress.

You still got it?

Of course I got it. She looks and sounds hurt so I kiss her. Maybe next week I'll go look at dresses. I want something that'll make me look good. Something that'll make my ass look good.

We head down a road for utility vehicles, where beer

bottles grow out of the weeds like squashes. The Hacienda is past this road, a house with orange tiles on the roof and yellow stucco on the walls. The boards across the windows are as loose as old teeth, the bushes around the front big and mangy like old school afros. When the cops nailed her here last year she told them she was looking for me, that we were supposed to be going to a movie together. I wasn't within ten miles of the place. Those pigs must have laughed their asses off. A movie. Of course. When they asked her what movie she couldn't even come up with one.

I want you to wait out here, she says.

That's fine by me. The Hacienda's not my territory.

Aurora rubs a finger over her chin. Don't go nowhere. Just hurry your ass up.

I will. She put her hands in her purple windbreaker.

Make it fast Aurora.

I just got to have a word with somebody, she says and I'm thinking how easy it would be for her to turn around and say, Hey, let's go home. I'd put my arm around her and I wouldn't let her go for like fifty years, maybe not ever. I know people who quit just like that, who wake up one day with bad breath and say, No more, I've had enough. She smiles at me and jogs around the corner, the ends of her hair falling up and down on her neck. I make myself a shadow against the bushes and listen for the Dodges and the Chevies that stop in the next parking lot, for the walkers that come rolling up with their hands in their pockets. I hear everything. A bike chain rattling. TVs snapping on in nearby apartments, squeezing ten voices into a room. After an hour the traffic on Route 9 has slowed and you can hear the cars roaring on from as far up as the Ernston light. Everybody knows about this house; people come from all over.

I'm sweating. I walk down to the utility road and come back. Come on, I say. An old fuck in a green sweatsuit comes out of the Hacienda, his hair combed up into a salt and pepper torch. An abuelo type, the sort who yells at you for spitting on his sidewalk. He has this smile on his face – big, wide, shit-eating. I know all about the nonsense that goes on in these houses, the ass that gets sold, the beasting.

Hey, I say and when he sees me, short, dark, unhappy, he breaks. He throws himself against his car door. Come here, I say. I walk over to him slow, my hand out in front of me like I'm armed. I just want to ask you something. He slides down to the ground, his arms out, fingers spread, hands like starfishes. I step on his ankle but he doesn't yell. He has his eyes closed, his nostrils wide. I grind down hard but he doesn't make a sound.

While You Were Gone

She sent me three letters from juvie and none of them said much, three pages of bullshit. She talked about the food and how rough the sheets were, how she woke up ashy in the morning, like it was winter. Three months and I still haven't had my period. The doctor here tells me it's my nerves. Yeah, right. I'd tell you about the other girls (there's a lot to tell) but they rip those letters up. I hope you doing good. Don't think bad about me. And don't let anybody sell my dogs either.

Her tía Fresa held onto the first letters for a couple of weeks before turning them over to me, unopened. Just tell me if she's OK or not, Fresa said. That's about as much as I want to know.

She sounds OK to me.

Good. Don't tell me anything else.

You should at least write her.

She put her hands on my shoulders and leaned down to my ear. You write her.

I wrote but I can't remember what I said to her, except that the cops had come after her neighbor for stealing somebody's car and that the gulls were shitting on everything. After the second letter I didn't write anymore and it didn't feel wrong or bad. I had a lot to keep me busy.

She came home in September and by then we had the Pathfinder in the parking lot and a new Zenith in the living room. Stay away from her, Cut said. Luck like that don't get better.

No sweat, I said. You know I got the iron will.

People like her got addictive personalities. You don't want to be catching that.

We stayed apart a whole weekend but on Monday I was coming home from Pathmark with a gallon of milk when I heard, Hey macho. I turned around and there she was, out with her dogs. She was wearing a black sweater, black stirrup pants and old black sneakers. I thought she'd come out messed-up but she was just thinner and couldn't keep still, her hands and face restless, like kids you have to watch.

How are you? I kept asking and she said, Just put your hands on me. We started to walk and the more we talked the faster we went.

Do this, she said. I want to feel your fingers.

She had mouth-sized bruises on her neck. Don't worry about them. They ain't contagious.

I can feel your bones.

She laughed. I can feel them too.

If I had half a brain I would have done what Cut told me to do. Dump her sorry ass. When I told him we were in love he laughed. I'm the King of Bullshit, he said, and you just hit me with some, my friend.

We found an empty apartment out near the highway, left the dogs and the milk outside. You know how it is when you get back with somebody you've loved. It felt better than it ever was, better than it ever could be again. After, she drew on the walls with her lipstick and her nail polish, stick men and stick women boning.

What was it like in there? I asked. Me and Cut drove past one night and it didn't look good. We honked the horn for a long time, you know, thought maybe you'd hear.

She sat up and looked at me. It was a cold-ass stare.

We were just hoping.

I hit a couple of girls, she said. Stupid girls. That was a big mistake. The staff put me in the Quiet Room. Eleven days the first time. Fourteen after that. That's the sort of shit that you can't get used to, no matter who you are. She looked at her drawings. I made up this whole new life in there. You should have seen it. The two of us had kids, a big blue house, hobbies, the whole fucking thing.

She ran her nails over my side. A week from then she would be asking me again, begging actually, telling me all the good things we'd do and after a while I hit her and made the blood come out of her ear like a worm but right then, in that apartment, we seemed like we were normal folks. Like maybe everything was better.

Aguantando

1

I lived without a father for the first nine years of my life. He was in the States, working, and the only way I knew him was through the photographs my moms kept in a plastic sandwich bag under her bed. Since our zinc roof leaked almost everything we owned was water stained: our clothes, Mami's Bible, her make-up, whatever food we had, Abuelo's tools, even our cheap wooden furniture. It was only because of that plastic bag that any pictures of my father survived.

When I thought of Papi I thought of one shot specifically. Taken days before the U.S. invasion. 1965. I wasn't even alive then; Mami had been pregnant with my first, never-born brother and Abuelo could still see well enough to hold a job. You know the sort of photograph I'm talking about. Scalloped edges, mostly brown in color. On the back my moms' cramped handwriting – the date, his name, even the street, one over from our house. He was dressed in his Guardia uniform, his tan cap at an angle on his shaved head, an unlit Constitución squeezed between his lips. His dark unsmiling eyes were my own.

I did not think of him often. He had left for Nueva York

when I was four but since I couldn't remember a single moment with him I excused him from all nine years of my life. On the days I had to imagine him – not often, since Mami didn't much speak of him anymore – he was the soldier in the photo. He was a cloud of cigar smoke, the traces of which could still be found on the uniforms he'd left behind. He was pieces of my friends' fathers, of the domino players on the corner, pieces of Mami and Abuelo. I didn't know him at all. I didn't know that he'd abandoned us. That this waiting for him was all a sham.

We lived south of the Cementerio Nacional in a wood-frame house with three rooms. We were poor. The only way we could have been poorer was to have lived in the campo or to have been Haitian immigrants, and Mami regularly offered these to us as brutal consolation.

At least you're not in the campo. You'd eat rocks then.

We didn't eat rocks but we didn't meat or beans, either. Almost everything on our plates was boiled: boiled yuca, boiled platano, boiled guineo, maybe with a piece of cheese or a shred of bacalao. On the best days the cheese and the platanos were fried. When me and Rafa caught our annual case of worms it was only by skimping on our dinners that Mami could afford to purchase the Verminox. I can't remember how many times I crouched over our latrine, my teeth clenched, watching long gray parasites sliding out from between my legs.

At Mauricio Baez, our school, the kids didn't bother us too much, even though we couldn't afford the uniforms or proper mascotas. The uniforms Mami could do nothing about but with the mascotas she improvised, sewing together sheets of loose paper she had collected from her friends. We each had one pencil and if we lost that pencil, like I did once, we had to stay home from school until Mami could borrow another one for us. Our professor had us share school books with some of the other kids and these kids wouldn't look at us, tried to hold their breath when we were close to them.

Mami worked at Embajador Chocolate, putting in ten-, twelve-hour shifts for almost no money at all. She woke up every morning at seven and I got up with her because I could never sleep late, and while she drew the water out of our steel drum I brought the soap from the kitchen. There were always leaves and spiders in the water but Mami could draw a clean bucket better than anyone. She was a tiny woman and in the watercloset she looked even smaller, her skin dark and her hair surprisingly straight and across her stomach and back the scars from the rocket attack she'd survived in 1965. None of the scars showed when she wore clothes, though if you embraced her you'd feel them hard under your wrist, against the soft part of your palm.

Abuelo was supposed to watch us while Mami was at work but usually he was visiting with his friends or out with his trap. A few years back, when the rat problem in the barrio had gotten out of hand (those malditos were running off with kids, Abuelo told me) he had built himself a trap. A destroyer. He never charged anyone for using it, something Mami would have done; his only commission was that he be the one to arm the steel bar. I've seen this thing chop off fingers, he explained to the borrowers but in truth he just liked having something to do, a job of some kind. In our house alone Abuelo had killed a dozen

rats and in one house on Tunti, forty of these motherfuck-
ers were killed during a two-night massacre. He spent
both nights with the Tunti people, resetting the trap and
burning the blood and when he came back he was grinning and tired, his white hair everywhere, and my mother
had said, You look like you've been out getting ass.

Without Abuelo around, me and Rafa did anything we
wanted. Mostly Rafa hung out with his friends and I
played with our neighbor Wilfredo. Sometimes I climbed
trees. There wasn't a tree in the barrio I couldn't climb and
on some days I spent entire afternoons in our trees, watching the barrio in motion and when Abuelo was around
(and awake) he talked to me about the good old days,
when a man could still make a living from his finca, when
the United States wasn't something folks planned on.

Mami came home after sunset, just when the day's
worth of drinking was starting to turn some of the neighbors wild. Our barrio was not the safest of places and
Mami usually asked one of her co-workers to accompany
her home. These men were young, and some of them were
even unmarried. Mami let them walk her but she never
invited them into the house. She barred the door with her
arm while she said good-bye, just to show them that
nobody was getting in. Mami might have been skinny, a
bad thing on the Island, but she was smart and funny and
that's hard to find anywhere. Men were drawn to her.
From my perch I'd watched more than one of these
Porfirio Rubirosas say, See you tomorrow, and then park
his ass across the street just to see if she was playing hard
to get. Mami never knew these men were there and after
about fifteen minutes of staring expectantly at the front of

our house even the loneliest of these fulanos put their hats on and went home.

We could never get Mami to do anything after work, even cook dinner, if she didn't first sit a while in her rocking chair. She didn't want to hear nothing about our problems, the scratches we'd put into our knees, who said what. She sat on the back patio with her eyes closed and let the bugs bite mountains onto her arms and legs. Sometimes I climbed the guanábana tree and when she opened her eyes and caught me smiling down on her, she closed them again and I dropped twigs onto her until she laughed.

2

When times were real flojo, when the last colored bill flew out Mami's purse, she packed us off to our relatives. She'd use Wilfredo's father's phone and make the calls early in the morning. Lying next to Rafa, I'd listen to her soft unhurried requests and pray for the day that our relatives would tell her to vete pa'l carajo but that never happened in Santo Domingo.

Usually Rafa stayed with our tíos in Ocoa and I went to tía Miranda's in Boca Chica. Sometimes we both went to Ocoa. Neither Boca Chica nor Ocoa were far but I never wanted to go and it normally took hours of cajoling before I agreed to climb on the autobus.

How long? I asked Mami truculently.

Not long, she promised me, examining the scabs on the back of my shaved head. A week. Two at the most.

How many days is that?

Ten, twenty.

You'll be fine, Rafa told me, spitting into the gutter.

57

How do you know? You a brujo?

Yeah, he said, smiling, that's me.

He didn't mind going anywhere; he was at that age when all he wanted was to be away from the family, meeting people he had not grown up with.

Everybody needs a vacation, Abuelo explained happily. Enjoy yourself. You'll be down by the water. And just think about all the food you'll eat.

I never wanted to be away from the family. Intuitively, I knew how easily distances could harden and become permanent. On the ride to Boca Chica I was always too depressed to notice the ocean, the young boys fishing and selling cocos by the side of the road, the surf exploding into the air like a cloud of shredded silver.

Tía Miranda had a nice block house, with a shingled roof and a tiled floor that her cats had trouble negotiating. She had a set of matching furniture and a television and faucets that worked. All her neighbors were administrators and hombres de negocios and you had to walk three blocks to find any sort of colmado. It was that sort of neighborhood. The ocean was never far away and most of the time I was down by the beach playing with the local kids, turning black in the sun.

Tía wasn't really related to Mami; she was my madrina, which was why she took me and my brother in every now and then. No money, though. She never loaned money to anyone, even to her drunkard of an ex-husband, and Mami must have known because she never asked. Tía was about fifty and rail thin and couldn't put anything in her hair to make it forget itself; her perms never lasted more than a week before the enthusiasm of her kink returned. She had two kids of her own, Yennifer and Bienvenido, but she didn't dote on them the way she doted on me. Her lips were always on me and during meals she watched me like she was waiting for the poison to take effect.

I bet this isn't something you've eaten lately, she'd say.

I'd shake my head and Yennifer, who was eighteen and bleached her hair, would say, Leave him alone, Mamá.

Tía also had a penchant for uttering cryptic one-liners about my father, usually after she'd downed a couple of shots of Brugal.

He took too much.

If only your mother could have noticed his true nature earlier.

He should see how he has left you.

The weeks couldn't pass quickly enough. At night I went down by the water to be alone but that wasn't possible. Not with the tourists making apes out of themselves, and with the tígueres waiting to rob them.

Las Tres Marías, I pointed out to myself in the sky. They were the only stars I knew.

But then one day I'd walk into the house from swimming and Mami and Rafa would be in the living room, holding glasses of sweet lemon-milk.

You're back, I'd say, trying to hide the excitement in my voice.

I hope he behaved himself, Mami would be saying to Tía. Her hair would be cut, her nails painted; she'd have on the same red dress she wore on every one of her outings.

Rafa smiling, slapping me on the shoulder, darker than I'd last seen him. How ya doing, Yunior? You miss me or what?

I'd sit next to him and he'd put his arm around me and we'd listen to Tía telling Mami how well I behaved and all the different things I'd eaten.

3

The year Papi came for us, the year I was nine, we expected nothing. There were no signs to speak of. Dominican chocolate was not especially in demand that season and the Puerto Rican owners laid off the majority of the employees for a couple of months. Good for the owners, un desastre for us. After that, Mami was around the house all the time. Unlike Rafa, who hid his shit well, I was always in trouble. From punching out Wilfredo to chasing somebody's chickens until they passed out from exhaustion. Mami wasn't a hitter; she preferred having me kneel on pebbles with my face against a wall. On the afternoon that the letter arrived, she caught me trying to stab our mango tree with Abuelo's machete. Back to the corner. Abuelo was supposed to make sure I served my ten minutes but he was too busy whittling to bother. He let me up after three minutes and I hid in the bedroom until he said OK, in a voice that Mami could hear. Then I went to the smokehouse, rubbing my knees and Mami looked up from peeling platanos. You better learn, muchacho, or you'll be kneeling the rest of your life.

I watched the rain that had been falling all day. No, I won't, I told her.

You talking back to me?

She whacked me on the nalgas and I ran outside to look for Wilfredo. I found him under the eaves of his house, the wind throwing pieces of rain onto his dark-dark face. We shook hands elaborately. I called him Muhammad Ali and he called me Sinbad; these were our North American names. We were both in shorts; a disintegrating pair of sandals clung to his toes.

What you got? I asked him.

Boats, he said, holding up the paper wedges his father had folded for us. This one's mine.

What does the winner get?

A gold trophy, about this big.

OK, cabrón, I'm in. Don't let go before me.

OK, he said, stepping to the other side of the gutter. We had a clear run down to the street corner. No cars were parked on our side, except for a drowned Monarch and there was plenty of room between its tires and the curb for us to navigate through.

We completed five runs before I noticed that somebody had parked their battered motorcycle in front of my house.

Who's that? Wilfredo asked me, dropping his soggy boat into the water again.

I don't know, I said.

Go find out.

I was already on my way. The motorcycle driver came out before I could reach our front door. He mounted quickly and was gone in a cloud of exhaust.

Mami and Abuelo were on the back patio, conversating. Abuelo was angry and his canecutter's hands were clenched. I hadn't seen Abuelo bravo in a long time, not since his produce truck had been stolen by two of his old employees.

Go outside, Mami told me.

Who was that?

Did I tell you something?

Was that somebody we know?

Outside, Mami said, her voice a murder about to happen.

What's wrong? Wilfredo asked me when I rejoined him. His nose was starting to run.

I don't know, I said.

When Rafa showed himself an hour later, swaggering in from a game of pool, I'd already tried to speak to Mami and Abuelo like five times. The last time Mami had landed a slap on my neck and Wilfredo told me that he could see the imprints of her fingers on my skin. I told it all to Rafa.

That doesn't sound good. He threw out his guttering cigarette. You wait here. He went around the back and I heard his voice and then Mami's. No yelling, no argument.

Come on, he said. She wants us to wait in our room.

Why?

That's what she said. You want me to tell her no?

Not while she's mad.

Exactly.

I slapped Wilfredo's hand and walked in the front door with Rafa. What's going on?

She got a letter from Papi.

Really? Is there money?

No.

What does it say?

How should I know?

He sat down on his side of the bed and produced a pack of cigarettes. I watched him go through the elaborate ritual of lighting up – the flip of the thin cigarrillo into his lips and then the spark, a single practiced snap of the thumb.

Where'd you get that lighter?

Mi novia gave it to me.

Tell her to give me one.

Here. He tossed it to me. You can have it if you shut up. Yeah?

See. He reached to take it. You already lost it.

I shut my mouth and he settled back down on the bed.

Hey, Sinbad, Wilfredo said, his head appearing in our window. What's going on?

My father wrote us a letter!

Rafa rapped me on the side of my head. This is a family affair, Yunior. Don't blab it all over the place.

Wilfredo smiled. I ain't going to tell anybody.

Of course you're not, Rafa said. Because if you do I'll chop your fucking head off.

I tried to wait it out. Our room was nothing more than a section of the house that Abuelo had partitioned off with planks of wood. In one corner Mami kept an altar with candles and a cigar in a stone mortar and a glass of water and two toy soldiers we could not touch ever and above the bed sprawled our mosquito netting. I lay back and listened to the rain brushing back and forth across our zinc roof.

Mami served dinner, watched as we ate it, and then ordered us back into our room. I'd never seen her so blank-faced, so stiff, and when I tried to hug her she pushed me away. Back to bed, she said. Back to listening to the rain. I must have fallen asleep because when I woke up Rafa was looking at me pensively and it was dark outside and nobody else in the house was awake.

I read the letter, he told me quietly. He was sitting cross-legged on the bed, his ribs laddering his chest in shadows.

Papi says he's coming, Rafa explained.

Really?

Don't believe it.

Why?

It ain't the first time he's made that promise, Yunior.

Oh, I said.

Outside Señora Tejada started singing to herself, badly.

Rafa?

Yeah?

I didn't know you could read.

I was nine and couldn't even write my own name.

Yeah, he said quietly. Something I picked up. Now go to bed.

4

Rafa was right. It wasn't the first time. Two years after he left, Papi wrote her saying he was coming for us and like an innocent Mami believed him. After being alone for two years she was ready to believe anything. She showed everybody his letter and even spoke to him on the phone. He wasn't an easy man to reach but on this occasion she got through and he reassured her that yes, he was coming. His word was his bond. He even spoke to us, something that Rafa vaguely remembers, a lot of crap about how much he loved us and that we should take care of Mami.

She prepared a party, even lined up to have a goat there for the slaughtering. She bought me and Rafa new clothes and when he didn't show she sent everybody home, sold the goat back to its owner and then almost lost her mind. I remember the heaviness of that month, thicker than almost anything. When Abuelo tried to reach our father at the phone numbers he'd left none of the men who'd lived with him knew anything about where he had gone.

It didn't help matters that me and Rafa kept asking her when we were leaving for the States, when Papi was coming. I am told that I wanted to see his picture almost every day. It's hard for me to imagine myself this way, crazy about Papi. When she refused to show me the photos I threw myself about like I was on fire. And I screamed. Even as a boy my voice carried farther than a man's, turned heads on the street.

First Mami tried slapping me quiet but that did little. Then she locked me in my room where my brother told me to cool it but I shook my head and screamed louder. I was inconsolable. I learned to tear my clothes because this was the one thing I had whose destruction hurt my mother. She took all my shirts from my room, left me only with shorts which were hard to damage with bare fingers. I pulled a nail from our wall and punched a dozen holes in each pair, until Rafa cuffed me and said, Enough, you little puto.

Mami spent a lot of time out of the house, at work or down by the Malecón, where she could watch the waves shred themselves against the rocks, where men offered cigarettes that she smoked quietly. I don't know how long this went on. Months, possibly three. Then, one morning in early spring, when the amapolas were flushed with their flame leaves, I woke up and found Abuelo alone in the house.

She's gone, he said. So cry all you want, malcriado.

I learned later from Rafa that she was in Ocoa with our tíos.

Mami's time away was never discussed, then or now.

65

When she returned to us, five weeks later, she was thinner and darker and her hands were heavy with calluses. She looked younger, like the girl who had arrived in Santo Domingo fifteen years before, the girl burning to be married. Her friends came and sat and talked and when Papi's name was mentioned her eyes dimmed and when his name left the darkness of her ojos returned and she would laugh, a small personal thunder that cleared the air.

She didn't treat me badly on her return but we were no longer as close; she did not call me her Prieto or bring me chocolates from her work. That seemed to suit her fine. And I was young enough to grow out of her rejection. I still had baseball and my brother. I still had trees to climb and lizards to tear apart.

5

The week after the letter came I watched her, almost unconsciously, from my trees. She ironed cheese sandwiches in paper bags for our lunch, boiled platanos for our dinner. Our dirty clothes were pounded clean in the concrete trough on the side of the outhouse. Every time she thought I was scrabbling too high in the branches she called me back to the ground. You ain't Spiderman, you know, she said, rapping the top of my head with her knuckles. On the afternoons that Wilfredo's father came over to play dominos and talk politics, she sat with him and Abuelo and laughed at their campo stories. She seemed more normal to me but I was careful not to provoke her. There was still something volcanic about the way she held herself.

On Saturday a late hurricane passed close to the Capital

and the next day folks were talking about how high the waves were down by the Malecón. Some children had been lost, swept out to sea and Abuelo shook his head when he heard the news. You'd think the sea would be tired of us by now, he said.

That Sunday Mami gathered us on the back patio. We're taking a day off, she announced. A day for us as a family.

We don't need a day off, I said and Rafa hit me harder than normal.

Shut up, OK?

I tried to hit him back but Abuelo grabbed us both by the arm. Don't make me have to crack your heads open, he said.

She dressed and put her hair up and even paid for a concho instead of crowding us into an autobus. The driver actually wiped the seats down with a towel while we waited and I said to him, It don't look dirty, and he said, Believe me, muchacho, it is. Mami looked beautiful and many of the men she passed wanted to know where she was heading. We couldn't afford it but she paid for a movie anyway. *The Five Deadly Venoms*. Kung-Fu movies were the only ones the theaters played in those days. I sat between Mami and Abuelo; Rafa moved to the back, joining a group of boys who were smoking and arguing with them about some baseball player on Licey.

After the show Mami bought us flavored ices and while we ate them we watched the salamanders crawling around on the sea rocks. The waves were tremendous and some parts of George Washington were flooded and cars were churning through the water slowly.

A man in a red guayabera stopped by us. He lit a cigarette

and turned to my mother, his collar turned up by the wind. So where are you from?

Santiago, she answered.

Rafa snorted.

You must be visiting relatives then.

Yes, she said. My husband's family.

He nodded. He was dark-skinned, with light-colored spots about his neck and hands. His finger trembled slightly as he worked the cigarette to his lips. I hoped he'd drop his cigarette, just so I could see what the ocean would do to it. We had to wait almost a full minute before he said buenos días and walked away.

What a crazy, Abuelo said.

Rafa lifted up his fist. You should have given me the signal. I would have Kung-Fu punched him in the head.

Your father came at me better than that, Mami said.

Abuelo stared down at the back of his hands, at the long white hairs that covered them. He looked embarrassed.

Your father asked me if I wanted a cigarette and then he gave me the whole pack to show me that he was a big man.

I held onto the rail. Here?

Oh no, she said. She turned around and looked out over the traffic. That part of the city isn't here anymore.

6

Rafa used to think that he'd come in the night, like Jesus, that one morning we'd find him at our breakfast table, unshaven and smiling. Too real to be believed. He'll be taller, Rafa predicted. North American food makes people that way. He'd surprise Mami on her way back from work, pick her up in a German car. Say nothing to the man walk-

68

ing her home. She would not know what to say and neither would he. They'd drive down to the Malecón and he'd take her to see a movie, because that's how they met and that's how he'd want to start it again.

I'd see him coming from my trees. A man with swinging hands and eyes like mine. He'd have gold on his fingers, cologne on his neck, a silk shirt, good leather shoes. The whole barrio would come out to greet him. He'd kiss Mami and Rafa and shake Abuelo's reluctant hand and then he'd see me behind everyone else. What's wrong with that one? he'd ask and Mami would say, He doesn't know you. Squatting down so that his pale yellow dress socks showed, he'd trace the scars on my arms and on my head. Yunior, he'd finally say, his stubbled face in front of mine, his fingers holding.

Drown

My mother tells me Beto's home, waits for me to say something, but I keep watching the TV. Only when she's in bed do I put on my jacket and swing through the neighborhood to see. He's a pato now but last year we were friends and he would walk into the apartment without knocking, his heavy voice rousing my mother from the Spanish of her room and drawing me up from the basement, a voice that crackled and made you think of uncles or grandfathers.

We were raging then, crazy the way we stole, broke windows, the way we pissed on people's steps and then challenged them to come out and stop us. Beto was leaving for college at the end of the summer and was delirious from the thought of it – he hated everything about the neighborhood, the break-apart buildings and he hated the dump, especially the dump.

I don't know how you can do it, he said to me. I would just find me a job anywhere and go.

Yeah, I said. I wasn't like him. I had another year to go in high school, no promises elsewhere.

Days we spent in the mall or out in the parking lot playing stickball, but nights were what we waited for. The heat in the apartments like something heavy that had come inside to die. Families arranged on their porches, the glow from their TVs washing blue against the brick. From my family apartment you could smell the pear trees that had been planted years ago, four to a court, probably to save us all from asphyxiation. Nothing moved fast, even the daylight was slow to fade, but as soon as night settled Beto and I headed down to the community center and sprang the fence into the pool. We were never alone, every kid with legs was there. We lunged from the boards and swam out of the deep end, wrestling and farting around. At around midnight abuelas, with their night hair swirled around spiky rollers, shouted at us from their apartment windows. Sinvergüenzas! Go home!

I pass his apartment but the windows are dark; I put my ear to the busted-up door and hear only the familiar hum of the air conditioner. I haven't yet decided if I'll talk to him. I can go back to my dinner and two years will become three.

Even from four blocks off I can hear the racket from the pool – radios too – and wonder if we were ever that loud. Little has changed, not the stink of chlorine, not the bottles exploding against the lifeguard station. I hook my fingers through the plastic-coated hurricane fence. Something tells me that he will be here; I hop the fence, feeling stupid when I sprawl on the dandelions and the grass.

Nice one, somebody calls out.

Fuck me, I say. I'm not the oldest motherfucker in the place, but it's close. I take off my shirt and my shoes and then knife in. Many of the kids here are younger brothers of the people I used to go to school with. Two of them swim past, black and Latino, and they pause when they see me, recognizing the guy who sells them their shitty dope. The crackheads have their own man, Lucero, and some other guy who drives in from Paterson, the only full-time commuter in the area.

The water feels good. Starting at the deep end I glide over the slick-tiled bottom without kicking up a spume or making a splash. Sometimes another swimmer churns past me, more a disturbance of water than a body. I can still go far without coming up. While everything above is loud and bright everything below is whispers. And always the risk of coming up to find the cops stabbing their searchlights out across the water. And then everyone running, wet feet slapping against the concrete, yelling, Fuck you, officers, you puto sucios, fuck you.

When I'm tired I wade through to the shallow end, past some kid who's kissing his girlfriend, watching me as though I'm going to try to cut in, and I sit near the sign that runs the pool during the day. No Horseplay, No Running, No Defecating, No Urinating, No Expectorating. At the bottom someone has scrawled in No Whites, No Fat Chiks and someone else has provided the missing c. I laugh. Beto hadn't known what expectorating meant though he was the one leaving for college. I told him, spitting a greener by the side of the pool.

Shit, he said. Where did you learn that?

I shrugged.

Tell me. He hated when I knew something he didn't. He put his hands on my shoulders and pushed me under. He was wearing a cross and cutoff jeans. He was stronger than me and held me down until water flooded my nose and throat. Even then I didn't tell him; he thought I didn't read, not even dictionaries.

*

73

We live alone. My mother has enough for the rent and gro-
ceries and I cover the phone bill, sometimes the cable.
She's so quiet that most of the time I'm startled to find her
in the apartment. I'll enter a room and she'll stir, detaching
herself from the cracking plaster walls, from the stained
cabinets, and fright will pass through me like a wire. She
has discovered the secret to silence: pouring café without a
splash, walking between rooms as if gliding on a cushion
of felt, crying without a sound. You have traveled to the
East and learned many secret things, I've told her. You're
like a shadow warrior.

And you're like a crazy, she says. Like a big crazy.

When I come in she's still awake, her hands picking
clots of lint from her skirt. I put a towel down on the sofa
and we watch television together. We settle on the Spanish-
language news: drama for her, violence for me. Today a
child has survived a seven-story fall, busting nothing but
his diaper. The hysterical baby-sitter, about 300 pounds of
her, is headbutting the microphone.

It's a Goddamn miraclevilla, she cries.

My mother asks me if I found Beto. I tell her that I
didn't look.

That's too bad. He was telling me that he might be starting at a school for business.

So what?

She's never understood why we don't speak anymore.
I've tried to explain, all wise-like, that everything changes,
but she thinks that sort of saying is only around so you can
prove it wrong.

He asked me what you were doing.

What did you say?

74

I told him you were fine.

You should have told him I moved.

And what if he ran into you?

I'm not allowed to visit my mother?

She notices the tightening of my arms. You should be more like me and your father.

Can't you see I'm watching television?

I was angry at him, wasn't I? But now we can talk to each other.

Am I watching television here or what?

Saturdays she asks me to take her to the mall. As a son I feel I owe her that much, even though neither of us has a car and we have to walk two miles through redneck territory to catch the M-15.

Before we head out she drags us through the apartment to make sure the windows are locked. She can't reach the latches so she has me test them. With the air conditioner on we never open windows but I go through the routine anyway. Putting my hand on the latch is not enough – she wants to hear it rattle. This place just isn't safe, she tells me. Lorena got lazy and look what they did to her. They punched her and kept her locked up in her place. Those morenos ate all her food and even made phone calls. Phone calls!

That's why we don't have long distance, I tell her but she shakes her head. That's not funny, she says.

She doesn't go out much, so when she does it's a big deal. She dresses up, even puts on make-up. Which is why I don't give her lip about taking her to the mall even though I usually make a fortune on Saturdays, selling to those kids going down to Belmar or out to Spruce Run.

I recognize like half the kids on the bus. I keep my head buried in my cap, praying that nobody tries to score. She watches the traffic, her hands somewhere inside her purse, doesn't say a word.

When we arrive at the mall I give her fifty dollars. Buy something, I say, hating the image I have of her, picking through the sale bins, wrinkling everything. Back in the day my father would give her a hundred dollars at the end of each summer for my new clothes and she would take nearly a week to spend it, even though it never amounted to more than a couple of T-shirts and two pairs of jeans. She folds the bills into a square. I'll see you at three, she says.

I wander through the stores, staying in sight of the cashiers so they won't have reason to follow me. The circuit I make has not changed since my looting days. Bookstore, record store, comic-book shop, Macy's. Me and Beto used to steal like mad from these places, two, three hundred dollars of gear in an outing. Our system was simple – we walked into a store with a shopping bag and came out loaded. Back then security wasn't tight. The only trick was in the exit. We stopped right at the entrance of the store and checked out some worthless piece of junk to stop people from getting suspicious. What do you think? we asked each other. Would she like it? Both of us had seen bad shoplifters at work. All grab and run, nothing smooth about them. Not us. We idled out of the stores slow, like a fat seventies car. At this, Beto was the best. He even talked to mall security, asked them for directions, his bag all loaded up, and me, standing ten feet away, shitting my pants. When he finished he smiled, swinging his shopping bag up to hit me.

You got to stop that messing around, I told him. I'm not going to jail for bullshit like that.

You don't go to jail for shoplifting. They just turn you over to your old man.

I don't know about you, but my pops hits like a motherfucker.

He laughed. You know my dad. He flexed his hands. The nigger's got arthritis.

My mother never suspected, even when my clothes couldn't all fit in my closet, but my father wasn't that easy. He knew what things cost and knew that I didn't have a regular job.

You're going to get caught, he told me one day. Just you wait. When you do I'll show them everything you've taken and then they'll throw your stupid ass away like a bad piece of meat.

He was a charmer, my pop, a real asshole, but he was right. Nobody can stay smooth forever, especially kids like us. One day at the bookstore, we didn't even hide the drops. Four issues of the same *Playboy* for kicks, enough Audio Books to start our own library. No last minute juke either. The lady who stepped in front of us didn't look old, even with her white hair. Her silk shirt was half-unbuttoned and a silver horn necklace sat on the freckled top of her chest. I'm sorry fellows, but I have to check your bag, she said. I kept moving, and looked back all annoyed, like she was asking us for a quarter or something. Beto got polite and stopped. No problem, he said, slamming the heavy bag into her face. She hit the cold tile with a squawk,

77

her palms slapping the ground. There you go, Beto said.

Security found us across from the bus stop, under a Jeep Cherokee. A bus had come and gone, both of us too scared to take it, imagining a plainclothes waiting to clap the cuffs on. I remember that when the rent-a-cop tapped his nightstick against the fender and said, You little shits better come out here real slow, I started to cry. Beto didn't say a word, his face stretched out and gray, his hand squeezing mine, the bones in our fingers pressing together.

Nights I drink with Alex and Danny. The Malibou Bar is no good, just washouts and the sucias we can con into joining us. We drink too much, roar at each other and make the skinny bartender move closer to the phone. On the wall hangs a cork dartboard and a Brunswick Gold Crown blocks the bathroom, its bumpers squashed, the felt pulled like old skin.

When the bar begins to shake back and forth like a rumba, I call it a night and go home, through the fields that surround the apartments. In the distance you can see the Raritan, as shiny as an earthworm, the same river my homeboy goes to school on. The dump has long since shut down, and grass has spread over it like a sickly fuzz, and from where I stand, my right hand directing a colorless stream of piss downward, the landfill might be the top of a blond head, square and old.

In the mornings I run. My mother is already up, dressing for her house-cleaning job. She says nothing to me, would rather point to the mangú she has prepared than speak.

I run three miles easily, could have pushed a fourth if I were in the mood. I keep an eye out for the recruiter who prowls around our neighborhood in his dark K-car. We've spoken before. He was out of uniform and called me over, jovial, and I thought I was helping some white dude with directions. Would you mind if I asked you a question?

No.

Do you have a job?

Not right now.

Would you like one? A real career, more than you'll get around here?

I remember stepping back. Depends on what it is, I said.

Son, I know somebody who's hiring. It's the United States Government.

Well. Sorry, but I ain't Army material.

That's exactly what I used to think, he said, his ten piggy fingers buried in his carpeted steering wheel. But now I have a house, a car, a gun, and a wife. Discipline. Loyalty. Can you say that you have those things? Even one?

He's a Southerner, red-haired, his drawl so out of place that the people around here laugh just hearing him. I take to the bushes when I see his car on the road. These days my guts feel loose and cold and I want to be away from here. He won't have to show me his Desert Eagle or flash the photos of the skinny Filipino girls sucking dick. He'll only have to smile and name the places and I'll listen.

When I reach the apartment, I lean against my door, waiting for my heart to slow, for the pain to lose its edge. I hear my mother's voice, a whisper from the kitchen. She sounds hurt or nervous, maybe both. At first I'm terrified that Beto's inside with her but then I look and see the phone cord, swinging lazily. She's talking to my father, something she knows I disapprove of. He's in Florida now, a sad guy who calls her and begs for money. He swears that if she moves down there he'll leave the woman he's living with. These are lies, I've told her but she still calls him. His words coil inside of her, wrecking her sleep for days. She opens the refrigerator door slightly so that the whir of the compressor masks their conversation. I walk in on her and hang up the phone. That's enough, I say.

She's startled, her hand squeezing the loose folds of her neck. That was him, she says quietly.

On school days Beto and I chilled at the stop together but as soon as that bus came over the Parkridge hill I got to thinking about how I was failing gym and screwing up math and how I hated every single living teacher on the planet.

I'll see you in the PM, I said.

He was already standing on line. I just stood back and grinned, my hands in my pockets. With our bus drivers you didn't have to hide. Two of them didn't give a rat fuck and the third one, the Brazilian preacher, was too busy talking Bible to notice anything but the traffic in front of him.

Being truant without a car was no easy job but I managed. I watched a lot of TV and when it got boring I trooped down to the mall or the Sayreville library, where you could watch old documentaries for free. I always came back to the neighborhood late, so the bus wouldn't pass me on Ernston and nobody could yell, Asshole! out the windows. Beto would usually be home or down by the swings, but other times he wouldn't be around at all. Out visiting other neighborhoods. He knew a lot of folks I didn't – a messed up black kid from Madison Park, two brothers who were into that NY club scene, who spent money on platform shoes and leather backpacks. I'd leave a message with his parents and then watch some more TV. The next day he would be out at the bus stop, too busy smoking a cigarette to say much about the day before.

You need to learn how to walk the world, he told me. There's a lot out there.

Some nights me and the boys drive to New Brunswick. A nice city, the Raritan so low and silty that you don't have to be Jesus to walk over it. We hit the Melody and the Roxy, stare at the college girls. We drink a lot and then spin out onto the dance floor. None of the chicas ever dance with us, but a glance or a touch can keep us talking shit for hours.

Once the clubs close we go to the Franklin Diner, gorge ourselves on pancakes, and then, after we've smoked our pack, head home. Danny passes out in the back seat and Alex cranks the window down to keep the wind in his eyes. He's fallen asleep in the past, wrecked two cars before this one. The streets have been picked clean of students and townies and we blow through every light, red or green. At the Old Bridge Turnpike we pass the fag bar, which never seems to close. Patos are all over the parking lot, drinking and talking.

Sometimes Alex will stop by the side of the road and say, Excuse me. When somebody comes over from the bar he will point his plastic pistol at them, just to see if they'll run or shit their pants. Tonight he just puts his head out the window. Fuck you! he shouts and then settles back in his seat, laughing.

That's original, I say.

He puts his head out the window again. Eat me, then!

Yeah, Danny mumbles from the back, Eat me.

Twice. That's it.

The first time was at the end of that summer. We had just come back from the pool and were watching a porn at his parents' apartment. His father was a nut for these videos, ordering them from wholesalers in California and Grand Rapids. Beto used to tell me how his pop would watch them in the middle of the day, not caring a lick about his moms, who spent the time in the kitchen, taking hours to cook a pot of rice and gandules. Beto would sit down with his pop and neither of them would say a word, except to laugh when somebody caught it in the eye or the face.

We were an hour into the new movie, some vaina that looked like it had been filmed in the apartment next door, when he reached into my shorts. What the fuck are you doing? I asked, but he didn't stop. His hand was dry. I kept my eyes on the television, too scared to watch. I came right away, smearing the plastic sofa covers. My legs started shaking and suddenly I wanted out. He didn't say anything to me as I left, just sat there watching the screen.

The next day he called and when I heard his voice I was cool but I wouldn't go to the mall or anywhere else. My mother sensed that something was wrong and pestered me about it but I told her to leave me the fuck alone, and my pops, who was home on a visit, stirred himself from his couch to slap me down. Mostly I stayed in the basement, terrified that I would end up abnormal, a fucking pato, but he was my best friend and back then that mattered to me more than anything. This alone got me out of the apartment and over to the pool. He was already there, his body pale and flabby under the water. Hey, he said. I was beginning to worry about you.

Nothing to worry about, I said.

We swam and didn't talk much and later we watched a Skytop crew pull a bikini top from a girl stupid enough to hang out alone. Give it, she said, covering herself, but these kids howled, holding it up over her head, the shiny laces flopping just out of reach. When they began to pluck at her arms, she walked away, leaving them to try the top on over their flat pecs.

He put his hand on my shoulder and my pulse a code under his palm. Let's go, he said. Unless of course you're not feeling good.

I'm feeling fine, I said.

Since his parents worked nights we pretty much owned the place until six the next morning. We sat in front of his television, in our towels, his hands bracing against my abdomen and thighs. I'll stop if you want, he said and I didn't respond. After I was done, he laid his head in my lap. I wasn't asleep or awake, but caught somewhere in between, rocked slowly back and forth the way surf holds junk against the shore, rolling it over and over. In three weeks he was leaving. Nobody can touch me, he kept saying. We'd visited the school and I'd seen how beautiful the campus was, with all the students drifting from dorm to class. I thought of how in high school our teachers loved to crowd us into their lounge every time a space shuttle took off from Florida. One teacher, whose family had two grammar schools named after it, compared us to the shuttles. A few of you are going to make it. Those are the orbiters. But the majority of you are just going to burn out. Going nowhere. He dropped his hand onto his desk. I could already see myself losing altitude, fading, the earth spread out beneath me, hard and bright.

I had my eyes closed and the television was on and when the hallway door crashed open, he jumped up and I nearly cut my dick off struggling with my shorts. It's just the neighbor, he said, laughing. He was laughing, but I was saying, Fuck this, and getting my clothes on.

I believe I see him in his father's bottomed-out Cadillac, heading towards the turnpike, but I can't be sure. He's probably back in school already. I deal close to home, trooping up and down the same dead-end street where the kids drink and smoke. These punks joke with me, pat me down for taps, sometimes too hard. Now that strip malls line Route 9, a lot of folks have part-time jobs; the kids stand around smoking in their aprons, name tags dangling heavily from pockets.

When I get home, my sneakers are filthy so I take an old toothbrush to their soles, scraping the crap into the tub. My mother has thrown open the windows and propped open the door. It's cool enough, she explains. She has prepared dinner – rice and beans, fried cheese, tostones. Look what I bought, she says, showing me two blue t-shirts. They were two for one so I bought you one. Try it on.

It fits tight but I don't mind. She cranks up the television. A movie dubbed into Spanish, a classic, one that everyone knows. The actors throw themselves around, passionate, but their words are plain and deliberate. It's hard to imagine anybody going through life this way. I pull out the plug of bills from my pockets. She takes it from me, her fingers soothing the creases. A man who treats his plata like this doesn't deserve to spend it, she says.

We watch the movie and the two hours together makes us friendly. She puts her hand on mine. Near the end of the film, just as our heroes are about to fall apart under a hail of bullets, she takes off her glasses and kneads her temples, the light of the television flickering across her face. She watches another minute and then her chin lists to her chest. Almost immediately her eyelashes begin to tremble, a quiet semaphore. She is dreaming, dreaming of Boca Raton, of strolling under the jacarandas with my father. You can't be anywhere forever was what Beto used to say, what he said to me the day I went to see him off. He handed me a gift, a book, and after he was gone I threw it away, didn't even bother to open it and read what he'd written.

I let her sleep until the end of the movie and when I wake her she shakes her head, grimacing. You better check those windows, she says. I promise her I will.

Boyfriend

I should have been careful with the weed. Most people it just fucks up. Me, it makes me sleepwalk. And wouldn't you know, I woke up in the hallway of our building, feeling like I'd been stepped on by my high school marching band. My ass would have been there all night if the folks in the apartment below hadn't been having themselves a big old fight at three in the morning. I was too fried to move, at least right away. Boyfriend was trying to snake Girlfriend, saying he needed space and she was like, Motherfucker, I'll give you all the space you need. I knew Boyfriend a little. I saw him at the bars and saw some of the girls he used to bring home while she was away. He just needed more space to cheat. Fine, he said, but every time he went for the door she got to crying and would be like, Why are you doing this? They sounded a lot like me and my old girlfriend Loretta, but I swore to myself that I would stop thinking about her ass, even though every Cleopatra-looking Latina in the City made me stop and wish she would come back to me. By the time Boyfriend got himself into the hallway I was already in my apartment. Girlfriend would not stop crying. Twice she stopped, she must have heard me moving around right above her and both times I held my breath until she started up again. I followed her into the bathroom, the two of us separated by a floor, wires and some pipes. She kept saying, Ese fucking pepetón, and washed her face over and over again. It would have broken my heart if it hadn't been so damn familiar. I guess I'd gotten numb to that sort of thing. I had heart-leather like walruses got blubber.

The next day I told my boy Harold what happened and he said too bad for her.

I guess so.

If I didn't have my own women problems I'd say let's go comfort the widow.

She ain't our type.

The hell she ain't.

Homegirl was too beautiful, too high class for a couple of knuckleheads like us. Never saw her in a T-shirt or without jewelry. And her boyfriend, olvidate. That nigger could have been a model; hell, they both could have been models, which was what they probably were considering that I never heard one word pass between them about a job or a fucking boss. People like these were Untouchables to me, raised on some other planet and then transplanted into my general vicinity to remind me how bad I was living. What was worse was how much Spanish they shared. None of my girlfriends ever spoke Spanish, even Loretta of the Puerto Rican attitudes. The closest thing for me was this black chick who spent three years in Italy. She liked to talk that shit in bed, and said she'd gone with me because I reminded her of some of the Sicilian men she'd known, which was why I never called her again.

Boyfriend came around a couple of times that week for his things and, I guess, to finish the job. He was a confident prick. He listened to what she had to say, arguments that had taken her hours to put together and then he would sigh, and say it didn't matter, he needed his space, punto. She let him fuck her every time, maybe hoping that it would make him stay but you know, once somebody gets a little escape velocity going, ain't no play in the world that will keep them from leaving. I would listen to them going at it and I would be like, Damn, ain't nothing more shabby than those farewell fucks. I know. Me and Loretta had enough of those to go around. Difference was, we never talked the way these two would. About our days. Not even when we were cool together. We'd lay there and listen to the world outside, to the loud boys, the cars, the pigeons. Back then I didn't have a clue what she was thinking but now I know what to pencil into all those empty thought bubbles. Escape. Escape.

These two had a thing about the bathroom. Each one of his visits ended up there. Which was fine by me, it was where I could hear them best. I don't know why I started following her life, but it seemed like a good thing to do. Most of the time I thought people, even at their worst, were pretty fucking boring. I guess I wasn't busy with anything else. Especially not women. I was taking time off, waiting for the last of my Loretta wreckage to drift out of sight.

The bathroom. Girlfriend talked a mile a minute about her day, how she saw a fistfight on the C train, how somebody liked her necklace and Boyfriend, with his smooth Barry White voice, just kept going Yeah. Yeah. Yeah. They'd shower together and if she wasn't talking she was going down on him. All you would hear down there was the water smacking the bottom of the tub and him going Yeah. Yeah. He wasn't sticking around, though. That was obvious. He was one of those dark-skinned smooth-faced brothers that women kill for and I knew for a fact, having seen his ass in action at the local spots, that he liked to get over on the whitegirls. She didn't know nothing about his little Rico Suave routine. It would have wrecked her. I used to think those were the barrio rules, Latinos and blacks in, whites out – a place we down cats weren't supposed to go. But love teaches you. Clears your head of any rules. Loretta's new boy was Italian, worked on Wall Street. When she told me about him we were still going out. We were on the Promenade and she said to me, I like him. He's a hard worker.

No amount of heart-leather could stop something like that from hurting.

After one of their showers, Boyfriend never came back. No phone calls, no nothing. She called a lot of her friends, ones she hadn't spoken to in the longest. I survived through my boys; I didn't have to call out for help. It was easy for them to say, Forget her sell-out ass. That's not the sort of woman you need. Look how light you are – no doubt she was already shopping for the lightest.

Mostly Girlfriend spent her time crying, either in the bathroom or in front of the TV. I spent my time listening and calling around for a job. Or smoking or drinking. A bottle of rum and two sixes of Presidente a week.

One night I got the cojones to ask her up for café, which was mighty manipulative of me. She hadn't had much human contact the whole month, except with the delivery guy from the Japanese restaurant, a Colombian dude I always said hi to, so what the hell was she going to say? No? She seemed glad to hear my name and when she threw open the door I was surprised to see her looking smart and watchful. She said she'd be right up and when she sat down across from me at the kitchen table she had on make-up and a rose-gold necklace.

You have a lot more light in your apartment than I do, she said.

Which was a nice call. About all I had in the apartment was light.

I played Andrés Jiménez for her – you know, *Yo quiero que mi Borinquen sea libre y soberana* – and then we drank a pot of café. El Pico, I told her. Nothing but the best. We didn't have much to talk about. She was depressed and tired and I had the worst gas of my life. Twice I had to excuse myself. Twice in an hour. She must have thought that bizarre as hell but both times I came out of the bathroom she was staring deeply into her café, the way the fortune tellers will do back on the Island. Crying all the time had made her more beautiful. Grief will do that sometimes. Not for me. Loretta had left months ago and I still looked like hell. Having Girlfriend in the apartment only made me feel shabbier. She picked up a cheeb seed from a crack in the table and smiled.

Do you smoke? I asked.

It makes me break out, she said.

Makes me sleepwalk.

Honey will stop that. It's an old Caribbean cure. I had a tío who would sleepwalk. One teaspoon a night took it out of him.

Wow, I said.

That night, she put on a freestyle tape, Nöel maybe, and I could hear her moving around her apartment. I wouldn't have put it past her to have been a dancer.

I never tried the honey and she never came back. Whenever I saw her on the stairs we would trade Hi's but she never slowed down to talk, never gave a smile or any other kind of encouragement. I took that as a hint. At the end of the month she got her hair cut short. No more straighteners, no more science fiction combs.

I like that, I told her. I was coming back from the liquor store and she was on her way out with a woman friend.

Makes you look fierce.

She smiled. That's exactly what I wanted.

Edison, New Jersey

The first time we try to deliver the Gold Crown the lights are on in the house but no one lets us in. I bang on the front door and Wayne hits the back and I can hear our double drum shaking the windows. Right then I have this feeling that someone is inside, laughing at us.

This guy better have a good excuse, Wayne says, lumbering around the newly-planted rose bushes. This is bullshit.

You're telling me, I say but Wayne's the one who takes this job too seriously. He pounds some more on the door, his face jiggling. A couple of times he raps on the windows, tries squinting through the curtains. I take a more philosophical approach; I walk over to the ditch that has been cut next to the road, a drainage pipe half filled with water, and sit down. I smoke and watch a mama duck and her three ducklings scavenge the grassy bank and then float downstream like they're on the same string. Beautiful, I say but Wayne doesn't hear. He's banging on the door with the staple gun.

At nine Wayne picks me up at the showroom and by then I have our route planned out. The order forms tell me everything I need to know about the customers we'll be dealing with that day. If someone is just getting a 52"card table delivered then you know they aren't going to give you too much of a hassle but they also aren't going to tip. Those are your Spotswood, Sayreville, and Perth Amboy deliveries. The pool tables go north to the rich suburbs – Livingston, Ridgewood, Bedminster. Also Long Island.

You should see our customers. Doctors, diplomats, surgeons, presidents of universities, ladies in slacks and silk tops who sport thin watches you could trade in for a car, who wear comfortable leather shoes. Most of them prepare for us by laying down a path of yesterday's *Washington Post* from the front door to the game room. I make them pick it all up. I say, Carajo, what if we slip? Do you know what two hundred pounds of slate could do to a floor? The threat of property damage puts the chop-chop in their step. The best customers leave us alone until the bill has to be signed. Every now and then we'll be given water in paper cups. Few have offered us more, though a dentist from Ghana once gave us a six-pack of Heineken while we worked.

Sometimes the customer has to jet to the store for cat food or a newspaper while we're in the middle of a job. I'm sure you'll be all right, they say. They never sound too sure. Of course, I say. Just show us where the silver's at. The customers ha-ha and we ha-ha and then they agonize over leaving, linger by the front door, trying to memorize everything they own, as if they don't know where to find us, who we work for.

Once they're gone, I don't have to worry about anyone bothering me. I put down the ratchet, crack my knuckles and explore, usually while Wayne is smoothing out the felt and doesn't need help. I take cookies from the kitchen, razors from the bathroom cabinets. Some of these houses have twenty, thirty rooms. I often count and on the ride back figure out how much loot it would take to fill up all that space. I've been caught roaming around plenty of times but you'd be surprised how quickly someone believes you're looking for the bathroom if you don't jump when you're discovered, if you just say, Hi.

After the paperwork's been signed, I have a decision to make. If the customer has been good and tipped well, we call it even and leave. If the customer has been an ass – maybe they yelled, maybe they let their kids throw golf balls at us – I ask for the bathroom. Wayne will pretend that he hasn't seen this before; he'll count the drill bits while the customer (or their maid) guides the vacuum over the floor. Excuse me, I say. I let them show me the way to the bathroom (usually I already know) and once the door is shut I cram bubble bath drops into my pockets and throw fist-sized wads of toilet paper into the toilet. I take a dump if I can and leave that for them.

Most of the time Wayne and I work well together. He's the driver and the money man and I do the lifting and handle the assholes. Tonight we're on our way to Lawrenceville and he wants to talk to me about Charlene, one of the show-room girls, the one with the blowjob lips. I haven't wanted to talk about women in months, not since the girlfriend.

I really want to pile her, he tells me. Maybe on one of the Madisons.

Man, I say, cutting my eyes towards him. Don't you have a wife or something?

He gets quiet. I'd still like to pile her, he says defensively. And what will that do?

Why does it have to do anything?

Twice this year Wayne's cheated on his wife and I've heard it all, the before and the after. The last time his wife nearly tossed his ass out to the dogs. Neither of the women seemed worth it to me. One of them was even younger than Charlene. Wayne can be a moody guy and this is one of those nights; he slouches in the driver's seat and swerves through traffic, riding other people's bumpers like I've told him not to do. I don't need a collision or a four-hour silent treatment so I try to forget that I think his wife is good people and ask him if Charlene's given him any signals.

He slows the truck down. Signals like you wouldn't believe, he says.

On the days we have no deliveries the boss has us working at the showroom, selling cards and poker chips and mankala boards. Wayne spends his time skeezing the salesgirls and dusting shelves. He's a big goofy guy – I don't understand why the girls dig his shit. One of those mysteries of the universe. The boss keeps me in the front of the store, away from the pool tables. He knows I'll talk to the customers, tell them not to buy the cheap models. I'll say shit like, Stay away from those Bristols. Wait until you can get something real. Only when he needs my Spanish will he let me help on a sale. Since I'm no good at cleaning or selling slot machines I slouch behind the front register and steal. I don't ring anything up, and pocket what comes in. I don't tell Wayne. He's too busy running his fingers through his beard, keeping the waves on his nappy head in order. A hundred buck haul's not unusual for me and back in the day, when the girlfriend used to pick me up, I'd buy her anything she wanted, dresses, silver rings, lingerie. Sometimes I blew it all on her. She didn't like the stealing but hell, we weren't made out of loot and I liked going into a place and saying, Jeva, pick out anything, it's yours. This is the closest I've come to feeling rich.

Nowadays I take the bus home and the cash stays with me. I sit next to this three hundred pound rock-and-roll chick who washes dishes at the Friendly's. She tells me about the roaches she kills with her water nozzle. Boils the wings right off them. On Thursday I buy myself lottery tickets – ten Quick Picks and a couple of Pick-Fours. I don't bother with the little stuff.

The second time we bring the Gold Crown the heavy curtain next to the door swings up like a Spanish fan. A woman stares at me and Wayne's too busy knocking to see. Muñeca, I say. She's black and unsmiling and then the curtain drops between us, a whisper on the glass. She had on a T-shirt that said No Problem and didn't look like she owned the place. She looked more like the help and couldn't have been older than twenty and from the thinness of her face I pictured the rest of her skinny. We stared at each other for a second at the most, not enough for me to notice the shape of her ears or if her lips were chapped. I've fallen in love on less.

Later in the truck, on the way back to the showroom Wayne mutters, This guy is dead. I mean it.

The girlfriend calls sometimes but not often. She has found herself a new boyfriend, some zángano who works at a record store. Dan is his name and the way she says it, so painfully gringo, makes the corners of my eyes narrow. The clothes I'm sure this guy tears from her when they both get home from work – the chokers, the rayon skirts from the Warehouse, the lingerie – I bought with stolen money and I'm glad that none of it was earned straining my back against hundreds of pounds of raw rock. I'm glad for that.

The last time I saw her in person was in Hoboken. She was with Dan and hadn't yet told me about him and hurried across the street in her high clogs to avoid me and my boys, who even then could sense me turning, turning into the motherfucker who'll put a fist through anything. She flung one hand in the air but didn't stop. A month before the zángano, I went to her house, a friend visiting a friend, and her parents asked me how business was, as if I balanced the books or something. Business is outstanding, I said.

That's really wonderful to hear, the father said.

You betcha.

He asked me to help him mow his lawn and while we were dribbling gas into the tank he offered me a job. A real one that you can build on. Utilities, he said, is nothing to be ashamed of.

Later the parents went to the den to watch the Giants lose and she took me into her bathroom. She put on her make-up because we were going to a movie. As friends. If I had your eyelashes, I'd be famous, she told me. The Giants started losing real bad. I still love you, she said and I was embarrassed for the two of us, the way I'm embarrassed at those afternoon talk shows where broken couples and unhappy families let their hearts hang out.

We're friends, I said and Yes, she said, yes we are.

There wasn't much space so I had to put my heels on the edge of the bathtub. The cross I'd given her dangled down on its silver chain so I put it in my mouth to keep it from poking me in the eye. By the time we finished my legs were bloodless, broomsticks inside my rolled-down baggies and as her breathing got smaller and smaller against my neck, she said, I do, I still do.

Each payday I take out the old calculator and figure how long it'd take me to buy a pool table honestly. A top of the line, three-piece slate affair doesn't come cheap. You have to buy sticks and balls and chalk and a score keeper and triangles and French tips if you're a fancy-shooter. Two and a half years if I give up buying underwear and eat only pasta but even this figure's bogus. Money's never stuck to me, ever.

Most people don't realize how sophisticated pool tables are. Yes, tables have bolts and staples on the rails but these suckers hold together mostly by gravity and by the precision of their construction. If you treat a good table right it will outlast you. Believe me. Cathedrals are built like that. There are Incan roads in the Andes that even today you couldn't work a knife between two of the cobblestones. The sewers that the Romans built in Bath were so good that they weren't replaced until the 1950s. That's the sort of thing I can believe in.

These days I can build a table with my eyes closed. Depending on how rushed we are I might build the table alone, let Wayne watch until I need help putting on the slate. It's better when the customers stay out of our faces, how they react when we're done, how they run fingers on the lacquered rails and suck in their breath, the felt so tight you couldn't pluck it if you tried. Beautiful, is what they say and we always nod, talc on our fingers, nod again, beautiful.

The boss nearly kicked our asses over the Gold Crown. The customer, an asshole named Pruitt, called up crazy, said we were *delinquent*. That's how the boss put it. Delinquent. We knew that's what the customer called us because the boss doesn't use words like that. Look boss, I said, we knocked like crazy. I mean, we knocked like Federal Marshals. Like Paul Bunyan. The boss wasn't having it. You fuckos, he said. You butthogs. He tore us for a good two minutes and then dismissed us. For most of that night I didn't think I had a job so I hit the bars, fantasizing that I would bump into this cabrón out with that black woman while me and my boys were cranked but the next morning Wayne came by with that Gold Crown again. Both of us had hangovers. One more time, he said. An extra delivery, no overtime. We hammered on the door for ten minutes but no one answered. I jimmied with the windows and the back door and I could have sworn I heard her behind the patio door. I knocked hard and footsteps, I heard footsteps.

We called the boss and told him what was what and the boss called the house but no one answered. OK, the boss said. Get those card tables done. That night, as we lined up the next day's paperwork, we got a call from Pruitt and he didn't use the word delinquent. He wanted us to come late at night but we were booked. Two-month waiting list, the boss reminded him. I looked over at Wayne and wondered how much money this guy was pouring into the boss's ear. Pruitt said he was *contrite* and *determined* and asked us to come again. His maid was sure to let us in.

What the hell kind of name is Pruitt anyway? Wayne asks me when we swing onto the Parkway.

Pato name, I say. Anglo or some other bog people.

Probably a fucking banker. What's the first name?

Just an initial, C. Clarence Pruitt sounds about right.

Yeah, Clarence, Wayne yuks.

Pruitt. Most of our customers have names like this, court case names: Wooley, Maynard, Gass, Binder, but the people from my town, our names, you see on convicts or coupled together on boxing cards.

We take our time. Go to the Rio Diner, blow an hour and all the dough we have in our pockets. Wayne is talking about Charlene and I'm leaning my head against a thick pane of glass.

Pruitt's neighborhood has recently gone up and only his court is complete. Gravel roams off this way and that, shaky. You can see inside the other houses, their newly-formed guts, nail heads bright and sharp on the fresh timber. Wrinkled blue tarps protect wiring and fresh plaster. The driveways are mud and on each lawn stands huge stacks of sod. We park in front of Pruitt's house and bang on the door. I give Wayne a hard look when I see no car in the garage.

Yes? I hear a voice inside say.

We're the delivery guys, I yell.

A bolt slides, a lock turns, the door opens. She stands in

our way, wearing black shorts and a gloss of red on her lips and I'm sweating.

Come in, yes? She stands back from the door, holding it open.

Sounds like Spanish, Wayne says.

No shit, I say, switching over. Do you remember me?

No, she says.

I look over at Wayne. Can you believe this?

I can believe anything, kid.

You heard us, didn't you? The other day, that was you.

She shrugs and opens the door wider.

You better tell her to prop that with a chair. Wayne heads back to unlock the truck.

You hold that door, I say.

We've had our share of delivery trouble. Trucks break down. Customers move and leave us with an empty house. Handguns get pointed. Slate gets dropped, a rail goes missing. The felt is the wrong color, the Dufferins get left in the warehouse. Back in the day the girlfriend and I made a game of this. A prediction game. In the mornings I rolled onto my pillow and said, What's today going to be like?

Let me check. She put her fingers up to her widow's peak and that motion would shift her breasts, her hair. We never slept under any covers, not in spring, fall, or summer and our bodies were dark and thin the whole year.

I see an asshole customer, she murmured. Unbearable traffic. Wayne's going to work slow. And then you'll come home to me.

Will I get rich?

You'll come home to me. That's the best I can do. And then we'd kiss hungrily because this was how we loved each other.

The game was part of our mornings, the way our showers and our sex and our breakfasts were. We stopped playing only when it started to go wrong for us, when I'd wake up and listen to the traffic outside without waking her, when everything was a fight.

She stays in the kitchen while we work. I can hear her humming. Wayne's shaking his right hand like he's scalded his fingertips. Yes, she's fine. She has her back to me, her hands stirring around in a full sink, when I walk in.

I try to sound conciliatory. You're from the city?

A nod.

Whereabout?

Washington Heights.

Dominicana, I say. Quisqueyana. She nods. What street?

I don't know the address, she says. I have it written down. My mother and my brothers live there.

I'm Dominican, I say.

You don't look it.

I get a glass of water. We're both staring out at the muddy lawn.

She says, I didn't answer the door because I wanted to piss him off.

Piss who off?

I want to get out of here, she says.

Out of here?

I'll pay you for a ride.

I don't think so, I said.

103

Aren't you from Nueva York?

No.

Then why did you ask the address?

Why? I have family near there.

Would it be that big of a problem?

I say in English that she should have her boss bring her but she stares at me blankly. I switch over.

He's a pendejo, she says, suddenly angry. I put down the glass, move next to her to wash it. She's exactly my height and smells of liquid detergent and has tiny beautiful moles on her neck, an archipelago leading down into her clothes.

Here, she says, putting out her hand but I finish it and go back to the den.

Do you know what she wants us to do? I say to Wayne.

Her room is upstairs, a bed, a closet, a dresser, yellow wallpaper. Spanish *Cosmo* and *El Diario* thrown on the floor. Four hangers worth of clothes in the closet and only the top dresser drawer is full. I put my hand on the bed and the cotton sheets are cool.

Pruitt has pictures of himself in his room. He's tan and probably has been to more countries than I know capitals for. Photos of him on vacations, on beaches, standing beside a wide-mouth Pacific salmon he's hooked. The size of his dome would have made Broca proud. The bed is made, his wardrobe spills out onto chairs and a line of dress shoes follows the far wall. A bachelor. I find an open box of Trojans in his dresser beneath a stack of boxer shorts. I put one of the condoms in my pocket and stick the rest under his bed.

I find her in her room. He likes clothes, she says.

A habit of money, I say but I can't translate it right; I end up agreeing with her. Are you going to pack?

She holds up her purse. I have everything I need. He can keep the rest of it.

You should take some of your things.

I don't care about that vaina. I just want to go.

Don't be stupid, I say. I open her dresser and pull out the jeans on top and a handful of soft bright panties fall out and roll down the front of my jeans. There are more in the drawer. I try to catch them but as soon as I touch their fabric I let everything go.

Leave it. Go on, she says and begins to put them back in the dresser, her square back to me, the movement of her hands smooth and easy.

Look, I say.

Don't worry. She doesn't look up.

I go downstairs. Wayne is sinking the bolts into the slate with the Makita. You can't do it, he says.

Why not?

We have to finish this.

I'll be back before you know it. A quick trip, in out.

Kid. He stands up slowly; he's nearly twice as old as me.

I go to the window and look out. New gingkoes stand in rows beside the driveway. A thousand years ago when I was still in college I learned something about them. Living fossils. Unchanged since their inception millions of years ago. You tagged Charlene, didn't you?

Sure did, he answers easily. I take the truck keys out of the tool box.

I'll be right back, I promise.

105

My mother still has pictures of the girlfriend in her apartment. The girlfriend's the sort of person who never looks bad. There's a picture of us at the bar where I taught her to play pool. She's leaning on the Schmelke I stole for her, nearly a grand worth of cue, frowning at the shot I left her, a shot she'd go on to miss.

The picture of us in Boca Raton is the biggest – shiny, framed, nearly a foot tall. We're in our bathing suits and the legs of some stranger frame the right. She has her butt in the sand, knees folded up in front of her because she knew I was sending the picture home to my mom; she didn't want my mother to see her bikini, didn't want my mother to think her a whore. I'm crouching next to her, smiling, one hand on her thin shoulder, one of her moles showing between my fingers.

My mother won't look at the pictures or talk about her when I'm around but my sister says she still cries over the break-up. Around me my mother's polite, sits quietly on the couch while I tell her about what I'm reading and how work has been. Do you have anyone? she asks me sometimes.

Yes, I say.

She talks to my sister on the side, says, In my dreams they're still together.

We reach the Washington Bridge without saying a word. She's emptied his cupboards and refrigerator; the bags are at her feet. She's eating corn chips but I'm too nervous to join in.

Is this the best way? she asks. The bridge doesn't seem to impress her.

It's the shortest way.

She folds the bag shut. That's what he said when I arrived last year. I wanted to see the countryside. There was too much rain to see anything anyway.

I want to ask her if she loves her boss, but I ask instead, How do you like the States?

She swings her head across at the the billboards. I'm not surprised by any of it, she says.

Traffic on the bridge is bad and she has to give me an oily fiver for the toll. Are you from the capital? I ask.

No.

I was born there. In Villa Juana. Moved here when I was a little boy.

She nods, staring out at the traffic. As we cross over the bridge I drop my hand into her lap. I leave it there, palm up, fingers slightly curled. Sometimes you just have to try, even if you know it won't work. She turns her head away slowly, facing out beyond the bridge cables, out to Manhattan and the Hudson.

Everything in Washington Heights is Dominican. You can't go a block without passing a Quisqueya Bakery or a Quisqueya Supermercado or a Hotel Quisqueya. If I were to park the truck and get out nobody would take me for a delivery man; I could be the guy who's on the street corner selling Dominican flags. I could be on my way home to my girl. Everybody's on the streets and the merengue's falling out of windows like TVs. When we reach her block I ask a kid with the sag for the building and he points out the stoop with his pinkie. She gets out of the truck and straightens the front of her sweatshirt before following the line that the kid's finger has cut across the street. Cuídate, I say.

*

107

Wayne works on the boss and a week later I'm back, on probation, painting the warehouse. Wayne brings me meatball sandwiches from out on the road, skinny things with a seam of cheese gumming the bread.

Was it worth it? he asks me.

He's watching me close. I tell him it wasn't.

Did you at least get some?

Hell yeah, I say.

Are you sure?

Why would I lie about something like that? Homegirl was an animal. I still have the teeth marks.

Damn, he says.

I punch him in the arm. And how's it going with you and Charlene?

I don't know, man. He shakes his head and in that motion I see him out on his lawn with all his things. I just don't know about this one.

We're back on the road a week later. Buckinghams, Imperials, Gold Crowns, and dozens of card tables. I keep a copy of Pruitt's paperwork and when the curiosity finally gets to me I call. The first time I get the machine. We're delivering at a house in Long Island with a view of the Sound that would break you. Wayne and I smoke a joint on the beach and I pick up a dead horseshoe crab by the tail and heave it in the customer's garage. The next two times I'm in the Bedminster area Pruitt picks up and says, Yes? But on the fourth time she answers and the sink is running on her side of the phone and she shuts it off when I don't say anything.

Was she there? Wayne asks in the truck.

Of course she was.

He runs a thumb over the front of his teeth. Pretty predictable. She's probably in love with the guy. You know how it is.

I sure do.

Don't get angry.

I'm tired, that's all.

Tired's the best way to be, he says. It really is.

He hands me the map and my fingers trace our deliveries, stitching city to city. Looks like we've gotten everything, I say.

Finally. He yawns. What's first tomorrow?

We won't really know until the morning, when I've gotten the paperwork in order but I take guesses anyway. One of our games. It passes the time, gives us something to look forward to. I close my eyes and put my hand on the map. So many towns, so many cities to choose from. Some places are sure bets but more than once I've gone with the long shot and been right.

You can't imagine how many times I've been right.

Usually the name will come to me fast, the way the numbered balls pop out during the lottery drawings, but this time nothing comes: no magic, no nothing. It could be anywhere. I open my eyes and see that Wayne is still waiting. Edison, I say, pressing my thumb down. Edison, New Jersey.

How to Date a Browngirl, Blackgirl, Whitegirl, or Halfie

Wait for your brother and your mother to leave the apartment. You've already told them that you're feeling too sick to go to Union City to visit that tía who likes to squeeze your nuts. (He's gotten big, she'll say.) And even though your moms knows you ain't sick you stuck to your story until finally she said, Go ahead and stay, malcriado.

Clear the government cheese from the refrigerator. If the girl's from the Terrace stack the boxes behind the milk. If she's from the Park or Society Hill hide the cheese in the cabinet above the oven, way up where she'll never see. Leave yourself a reminder to get it out before morning or your moms will kick your ass. Take down any embarrassing photos of your family in the campo, especially the one with the half-naked kids dragging a goat on a rope leash. The kids are your cousins and by now they're old enough to understand why you're doing what you're doing. Hide the pictures of yourself with an Afro. Make sure the bathroom is presentable. Put the basket with all the crapped-on toilet paper under the sink. Spray the bucket with Lysol, then close the cabinet.

Shower, comb, dress. Sit on the couch and watch TV. If she's an outsider her father will be bringing her, maybe her

111

mother. Neither of them want her seeing any boys from the Terrace – people get stabbed in the Terrace – but she's strong headed and this time will get her way. If she's a whitegirl you know you'll at least get a handjob.

The directions were in your best handwriting, so her parents won't think you're an idiot. Get up from the couch and check the parking lot. Nothing. If the girl's local, don't sweat it. She'll flow over when she's good and ready. Sometimes she'll run into her other friends and a whole crowd will show up at your apartment and even though that means you ain't getting shit it will be fun anyway and you'll wish these people would come over more often. Sometimes the girl won't flow over at all and the next day in school she'll say sorry, smile, and you'll be stupid enough to believe her and ask her out again.

Wait and after an hour go out to your corner. The neighborhood is full of traffic. Give one of your boys a shout and when he says, Are you still waiting on that bitch? say, Hell yeah.

Get back inside. Call her house and when her father picks up ask if she's there. He'll ask, who is this? Hang up. He sounds like a principal or a police chief, the sort of dude with a big neck who never has to watch his back. Sit and wait. By the time your stomach's ready to give out on you a Honda or maybe a Jeep pulls in and out she comes.

Hey, you'll say.

Look, she'll say. My mom wants to meet you. She's got herself all worried about nothing.

Don't panic. Say, Hey, no problem. Run a hand through your hair like the whiteboys do even though the only thing that runs easily through your hair is Africa. She will look good. The white ones are the ones you want the most, aren't they, but usually the out-of-towners are black, black-girls who grew up with ballet and girl scouts, who have three cars in their driveways. If she's a halfie don't be surprised that her mother is white. Say, Hi. Her moms will say hi and you'll see that you don't scare her, not really. She will say that she needs easier directions to get out and even though she has the best directions in her lap give her new ones. Make her happy.

You have choices. If the girl's from around the way, take her to El Cibao for dinner. Order everything in your busted-up Spanish. Let her correct you if she's Latina and amaze her if she's black. If she's not from around the way, Wendy's will do. As you walk to the restaurant talk about school. A local girl won't need stories about the neighborhood but the other ones might. Supply the story about the loco who'd been storing canisters of tear gas in his basement for years, how one day the canisters cracked and the whole neighborhood got a dose of the military strength stuff. Don't tell her that your moms knew right away what it was, that she recognized its smell from the year the United States invaded your island.

Hope that you don't run into your nemesis, Howie, the Puerto Rican kid with the two killer mutts. He walks them all over the neighborhood and every now and then the mutts corner themselves a cat and tear it to shreds, Howie laughing as the cat flips up in the air, its neck twisted around like an owl, red meat showing through the soft fur. If his dogs haven't cornered a cat, he will walk behind you and ask, Hey, Yunior, is that your new fuckbuddy?

Let him talk. Howie weighs about two hundred pounds

and could eat you if he wanted. At the field he will turn away. He has new sneakers, and doesn't want them muddy. If the girl's an outsider she will hiss now and say, What a fucking asshole. A homegirl would have been yelling back at him the whole time, unless she was shy. Either way don't feel bad that you didn't do anything. Never lose a fight on a first date or that will be the end of it.

Dinner will be tense. You are not good at talking to people you don't know. A halfie will tell you that her parents met in the Movement, will say, Back then people thought it a radical thing to do. It will sound like something her parents made her memorize. Your brother once heard that one and said, Man, that sounds like a whole lot of Uncle Tomming to me. Don't repeat this.

Put down your hamburger and say, It must have been hard.

She will appreciate your interest. She will tell you more. Black people, she will say, treat me real bad. That's why I don't like them. You'll wonder how she feels about Dominicans. Don't ask. Let her speak on it and when you're both finished eating walk back into the neighborhood. The skies will be magnificent. Pollutants have made Jersey sunsets one of the wonders of the world. Point it out. Touch her shoulder and say, That's nice, right?

Get serious. Watch TV but stay alert. Sip some of the Bermudez your father left in the cabinet, which nobody touches. A local girl may have hips and a thick ass but she won't be quick about letting you touch. She has to live in the same neighborhood you do, has to deal with you being all up in her business. She might just chill with you and then go home. She might kiss you and then go, or she might, if she's reckless, give it up, but that's rare. Kissing will suffice. A whitegirl might just give it up right then. Don't stop her. She'll take her gum out of her mouth, stick it to the plastic sofa covers and then will move close to you. You have nice eyes, she might say.

Tell her that you love her hair, that you love her skin, her lips, because, in truth, you love them more than you love your own.

She'll say, I like Spanish guys, and even though you've never been to Spain, say, I like you. You'll sound smooth.

You'll be with her until about 8:30 and then she will want to wash up. In the bathroom she will hum a song from the radio and her waist will keep the beat against the lip of the sink. Imagine her old lady coming to get her, what she would say if she knew her daughter had just lain under you and blown your name, pronounced with her eighth-grade Spanish, into your ear. While she's in the bathroom call one of your boys and say, Lo hice, cabrón. Or just sit back on the couch and smile.

But usually it won't work this way. Be prepared. She will not want to kiss you. Just cool it, she'll say. The halfie might lean back, breaking away from you. She will cross her arms, say, I hate my tits. Stroke her hair but she will pull away. I don't like anybody touching my hair, she will say. She will act like somebody you don't know. In school she is known for her attention-grabbing laugh, as high and far-ranging as a gull, but here she will worry you. You will not know what to say.

You're the only kind of guy who asks me out, she will say. Your neighbors will start their hyena-calls, now that the alcohol is in them. You and the black boys.

Say nothing. Let her button her shirt, let her comb her hair, the sound of it stretching like a sheet of fire between you. When her father pulls in and beeps, let her go without too much of a good-bye. She won't want it. During the next hour the phone will ring. You will be tempted to pick it up. Don't. Watch the shows you want to watch, without a family around to debate you. Don't go downstairs. Don't fall asleep. It won't help. Put the government cheese back in its place before your mom kills you.

No Face

In the morning he pulls on his mask and grinds his fist into his palm. He goes to the guanábana tree and does his pull ups, nearly fifty now, and then he picks up the café dehuller and holds it to his chest for a forty count. His arms, chest and neck bulge and the skin around his temple draws tight, about to split. But no! He's unbeatable and drops the dehuller with a fat Yes. He knows that he should go but the morning fog covers everything and he listens to the roosters for a while. Then he hears his family stirring. Hurry up, he says to himself. He runs past his tío's land and with a glance he knows how many beans of café his tío has growing red, black, and green on his conucos. He runs past the water hose and the pasture, and then he says FLIGHT and jumps up and his shadow knifes over the tops of the trees and he can see his family's fence and his mother washing his little brother, scrubbing his face and his feet.

The storekeepers toss water on the road to keep the dust down; he sweeps past them. No Face! a few yell out but he has no time for them. First he goes to the bars, searches the nearby ground for dropped change. Drunks sometimes sleep in the alleys so he moves quietly. He steps over the piss-holes and the vomit, wrinkles his nose at the

117

stink. Today he finds enough coins in the tall crackling weeds to buy a bottle of soda or a johnnycake. He holds the coins tightly in his hands and under his mask he smiles.

At the hottest part of the day Lou lets him into the church with its bad roof and poor wiring and gives him café con leche and two hours of reading and writing. The books, the pen, the paper all come from the nearby school, donated by the teacher. Father Lou has small hands and bad eyes and twice he's gone to Canada for operations. Lou teaches him the English he'll need up North. I'm hungry. Where's the bathroom? I come from the Dominican Republic. Don't be scared.

After his lessons he buys Chiclets and goes to the house across from the church. The house has a gate and orange trees and a cobblestone path. A TV trills somewhere inside. He waits for the girl but she doesn't come out. Normally she'd peek out and see him. She'd make a TV with her hands. They both speak with their hands.

Do you want to watch?

He'd shake his head, put his hands out in front of him. He never went into casas ajenas. No, I like being outside.

I'd rather be inside where it's cool.

He'd stay until the cleaning woman, who also lived in the mountains, yelled from the kitchen, Stay away from here. Don't you have any shame? Then he'd grip the bars of the gate and pull them a bit apart, grunting, to show her who she was messing with.

Each week Padre Lou lets him buy a comic book. The priest takes him to the bookseller and stands in the street, guarding him, while he peruses the shelves.

Today he buys Kaliman, who takes no shit and wears a turban. If his face was covered he'd be perfect.

He watches for opportunities from corners, away from people. He has his power of INVISIBILITY and no one can touch him. Even his tío, the one who guards the dams, strolls past and says nothing. Dogs can smell him though and a couple nuzzle his feet. He pushes them away since they can betray his location to his enemies. So many wish him to fall. So many wish him gone.

A viejo needs help pushing his cart. A cat needs to be brought across the street.

Hey No Face! a motor driver yells. What the hell are you doing? You haven't started eating cats, have you?

He'll be eating kids next, another joins in.

Leave that cat alone, it's not yours.

He runs. It's late in the day and the shops are closing and even the motor bikes at each corner have dispersed, leaving oil stains and ruts in the dirt.

The ambush comes when he's trying to figure out if he can buy another johnnycake. Four boys tackle him and the coins jump out of his hand like grasshoppers. The fat boy with the single eyebrow sits on his chest and his breath flies out of him. The others stand over them and he's scared.

We're going to make you a girl, the fat one says and he can hear the words echoing through the meat of the fat boy's body. He wants to breathe but his lungs are as tight as pockets.

You ever been a girl before?

I betcha he hasn't. It ain't a lot of fun.

He says STRENGTH and the fat boy flies off him and he's running down the street and the others are following. You better leave him alone, the owner of the beauty shop says but no one ever listens to her, not since her husband left her for a Haitian. He makes it back to the church and slips inside and hides. The boys throw rocks against the door of the church but then Eliseo, the groundskeeper says, Boys, prepare for hell, and runs his machete on the sidewalk. Everything outside goes quiet. He sits down under a pew and waits for night time, when he can go back home to the smokehouse to sleep. He rubs the blood on his shorts, spits on the cut to get the dirt out.

Are you okay? Padre Lou asks.

I've been running out of energy.

Padre Lou sits down. He looks like one of those Cuban shopkeepers in his shorts and guayabera. He pats his hands together. I've been thinking about you up North. I'm trying to imagine you in the snow.

Snow won't bother me.

Snow bothers everybody.

Do they like wrestling?

Padre Lou laughs. Almost as much as we do. Except nobody gets cut up, not anymore.

He comes out from under the pew then and shows the priest his elbow. The priest sighs. Let's go take care of that, OK.

Just don't use the red stuff.

We don't use the red stuff anymore. We have the white stuff now and it doesn't hurt.

I'll believe that when I see it.

*

No one has ever hidden it from him. They tell him the story over and over again, as though afraid that he might forget.

On some nights he opens his eyes and the pig has come back. Always huge and pale. Its hooves peg his chest down and he can smell the curdled bananas on its breath. Blunt teeth rip a strip from under his eye and the muscle revealed is delicious, like lechosa. He turns his head to save one side of his face; in some dreams he saves his right side and in some his left but in the worst ones he cannot turn his head or its mouth is like a pothole and nothing can escape it. When he awakens he's screaming and blood braids down his neck; he's bitten his tongue and it swells and he cannot sleep again until he tells himself to be a man.

Padre Lou borrows a Honda motorcycle and the two set out early in the morning. He leans into the turns and Lou says, Don't do that too much. You'll tip us.

Nothing will happen to us! he yells.

The road to Ocoa is empty and the fincas are dry and many of the farmsteads have been abandoned. On a bluff he sees a single black horse. It's eating a shrub and a garza is perched on its back.

The clinic is crowded with bleeding people but a nurse with bleached hair brings them through to the front.

How are we today? the doctor says.

I'm fine, he says. When are you sending me away?

The doctor smiles and makes him remove his mask and then massages his face with his thumbs. The doctor has colorless food in his teeth. Have you had trouble swallowing?

No.

Breathing?

121

No.

Have you had any headaches? Does your throat ever hurt? Are you ever dizzy?

Never.

The doctor checks his eyes, his ears, and then listens to his breathing. Everything looks good, Lou.

I'm glad to hear that. Do you have a ballpark figure?

Well, the doctor says. We'll get him there eventually.

Padre Lou smiles and puts a hand on his shoulder. What do you think about that?

He nods but doesn't know what he should think. He's scared of the operations and scared that nothing will change, that the Canadian doctors will fail like the santeras his mother hired, who called every spirit in the celestial directory for help. The room he's in is hot and dim and dusty and he's sweating and wishes he could lie under a table where no one can see. In the next room he met a boy whose skull plates had not closed all the way and a girl who didn't have arms and a baby whose face was huge and swollen and whose eyes were dripping pus.

You can see my brain, the boy said. All I have is this membrane thing and you can see right into it.

In the morning he wakes up hurting. From the doctor, from a fight he had outside the church. He goes outside, dizzy, and leans against the guanábana tree. His little brother Pesao is awake, flicking beans at the chickens, his little body bowed and perfect and when he rubs the four-year-old's head he feels the sores that have healed into yellow crusts. He aches to pick at them but the last time the blood had gushed and Pesao had screamed.

Where have you been? Pesao asks.

I've been fighting evil.

I want to do that.

You won't like it, he says.

Pesao looks at his face, giggles, and flings another pebble at the hens, who scatter indignantly.

He watches the sun burn the mists from the fields and despite the heat the beans are thick and green and flexible in the breeze. His mother sees him on the way back from the outhouse. She goes to fetch his mask.

He's tired and aching but he looks out over the valley and the way the land curves away to hide itself reminds him of the way Lou hides his dominos when they play. Go, she says. Before your father comes out.

He knows what happens when his father comes out. He pulls on his mask and feels the fleas stirring in the cloth. When she turns her back, he hides, blending into the weeds. He watches his mother hold Pesao's head gently under the faucet and when the water finally urges out from the pipe Pesao yells as if he's been given a present or a wish come true.

He runs, down towards town, never slipping or stumbling. Nobody's faster.

Negocios

My father, Ramón de las Casas, left Santo Domingo just before my fourth birthday. Papi had been planning to leave for months, hustling and borrowing from his friends, from anyone he could put the bite on. In the end it was just plain luck that got his visa processed when it did. The last of his luck on the Island, considering that Mami had recently discovered he was keeping with an overweight puta he had met while breaking up a fight on her street in Los Millonitos. Mami learned this from a friend of hers, a nurse and a neighbor of the puta. The nurse couldn't understand what Papi was doing loafing around her street when he was supposed to be on patrol.

The initial fights, with Mami throwing our silverware into wild orbits, lasted a week. After a fork pierced him in the cheek, Papi decided to move out, just until things cooled down. He took a small bag of clothes and broke out early in the morning. On his second night away from the house, with the puta asleep at his side, Papi had a dream that the money Mami's father had promised him was spiraling away in the wind like bright bright birds. The dream blew him out of bed like a gunshot. Are you OK? the puta asked and he shook his head. I think I have to go somewhere, he said. He borrowed a clean mustard-colored guayabera from a friend, put himself in a concho and paid our abuelo a visit.

Abuelo had his rocking chair in his usual place, out on the sidewalk where he could see everyone and everything. He had fashioned that chair as a thirtieth birthday present to himself and twice had to replace the wicker screens that his ass and shoulders had worn out. If you were to walk down to the Duarte you would see that type of chair for sale everywhere. It was November, the mangoes were thudding from the trees. Despite his dim eyesight, Abuelo saw Papi coming the moment he stepped onto Sumner Welles. Abuelo sighed, he'd had it up to his cojones with this spat. Papi hiked up his pants and squatted down next to the rocking chair.

I am here to talk to you about my life with your daughter, he said, removing his hat. I don't know what you've heard but I swear on my heart that none of it is true. All I want for your daughter and our children is to take them to the United States. I want a good life for them.

Abuelo searched his pockets for the cigarette he had just put away. The neighbors were gravitating towards the front of their houses to listen to all the exchange. What about this other woman? Abuelo said finally, unable to find the cigarette tucked behind his ear.

It's true I went to her house, but that was a mistake. I did nothing to shame you, viejo. I know it wasn't a smart thing to do, but I didn't know the woman would lie like she did.

Is that what you said to Virta?

Yes, but she won't listen. She cares too much about what she hears from her friends. If you don't think I can

126

do anything for your daughter then I won't ask to borrow that money.

Abuelo spit the taste of car exhaust and street dust from his mouth. He might have spit four or five times. The sun could have set twice on his deliberations but with his eyes quitting, his farm in Azua now dust, and his familia in need, what could he really do?

Listen Ramón, he said, scratching his arm hairs. I believe you. But Virta, she hears the chisme on the street and you know how that is. Come home and be good to her. Don't yell. Don't hit the children. I'll tell her that you are leaving soon. That will help smooth things between the two of you.

Papi fetched his things from the puta's house and moved back in that night. Mami acted as if he were a troublesome visitor who had to be endured. She slept with the children and stayed out of the house as often as she could, visiting her relatives in other parts of the Capital. Many times Papi took hold of her arms and pushed her against the slumping walls of the house, thinking his touch would snap her from her brooding silence, but instead she slapped or kicked him. Why the hell do you do that? he demanded. Don't you know how soon I'm leaving?

Then go, she said.

You'll regret that.

She shrugged and said nothing else.

In a house as loud as ours, one woman's silence was a palpable thing. Papi slouched about for a month, taking us to Kung-Fu movies we couldn't understand and drilling into us how we'd miss him. He'd hover around Mami while she checked our hair for lice, wanting to be nearby the instant she cracked and begged him to stay.

One night Abuelo handed Papi a cigar box stuffed with cash. The bills were new and smelled of ginger. Here it is. Make your children proud.

You'll see. He kissed the viejo's cheek and the next day had himself a ticket for a flight leaving in three days. He held the ticket in front of Mami's eyes. Do you see this?

She nodded tiredly and took up his hands. In their room, she already had his clothes packed and mended.

She didn't kiss him when he left. Instead she sent each of the children over to him. Say good-bye to your father. Tell him that you want him back soon.

When he tried to embrace her she grabbed his upper arms, her fingers like pincers. You had best remember where this money came from, she said, the last words they exchanged face to face for five years.

He arrived in Miami at four in the morning in a roaring poorly-booked plane. He passed easily through customs, having brought nothing but some clothes, a towel, a bar of soap, a razor, his money, and a box of Chiclets in his pocket. The ticket to Miami had saved him money but he intended to continue on to Nueva York as soon as he could. Nueva York was the city of jobs, the city that had first called the Cubanos and their cigar industry, then the Bootstrap Puertoricans and now called him.

He had trouble finding his way out of the terminal. Everyone was speaking English and the signs were no help. He smoked half a pack of cigarettes while wandering around. When he finally exited the terminal, he rested his bag on the sidewalk and threw away the rest of the cigarettes. In the darkness he could see little of North America. A vast stretch of cars, distant palms and a highway that reminded him of the Máximo Gómez. The air was not as hot as home and the city was well-lit but he didn't feel as if he had crossed an ocean and a world. A cab driver in front of the terminal called to him in Spanish and threw his bag easily in the back seat of the cab. A new one, he said. The man was black, stooped, and strong.

You got family here?

Not really.

How about an address?

Nope, Papi said. I'm here on my own. I got two hands and a heart as strong as a rock.

Right, the taxi driver said. He toured Papi through the city, around Calle Ocho. Although the streets were empty and accordion gates stretched in front of storefronts Papi recognized the prosperity in the buildings and in the tall operative lamp posts. He indulged himself in the feeling that he was being shown his new digs to insure that they met with his approval. Find a place to sleep here, the driver advised. And first thing tomorrow get yourself a job. Anything you can find.

I'm here to work.

Sure, said the driver. He dropped Papi off at a hotel and charged him five dollars for half an hour of service. Whatever you save on me will help you later. I hope you do well.

Papi offered the driver a tip but the driver was already pulling away, the dome atop his cab glowing, calling another fare. Shouldering his bag, Papi began to stroll, smelling the dust and the heat filtering up from the pressed rock of the streets. At first he considered saving money by sleeping outside on a bench but he was without guides and the inscrutability of the nearby signs unnerved him. What if there was a curfew? He knew that the slightest turn of fortune could dash him. How many before him had gotten this far only to get sent back for some stupid infraction? The sky was suddenly too high. He walked back the way he had come and went into the hotel, its spastic neon sign obtrusively jutting into the street. He had difficulty understanding the slender man at the desk, but finally the man wrote down the amount for a night's stay in block numbers. Room cuatro-cuatro, the man said. Papi had as much difficulty working the shower but finally was able to take a bath. It was the first bathroom he'd been in that hadn't curled the hair on his body. With the radio tuned in and incoherent, he trimmed his mustache. No photos exist of his mustache days but it is easily imagined. Within an hour he was asleep. He was twenty-four. He was strong. He didn't dream about his familia and wouldn't for many years. He dreamed instead about gold coins, like the ones that had been salvaged from the many wrecks about our Island, stacked high as sugarcane.

Even on his first disorienting morning, as an aged Latina snapped the sheets from the bed and emptied the one piece of scrap paper he'd thrown in the trash can, Papi pushed himself through the sit-ups and push-ups that kept him kicking ass until his forties.

You should try these, he told the Latina. They make work a lot easier.

If you had a job, she said. You wouldn't need exercise.

He stored the clothes he had worn the day before in his canvas shoulder bag and assembled a new outfit. He used his fingers and water to flatten out the worst of the wrinkles. During the years he'd lived with Mami, he'd washed and ironed his own clothes. These things were a man's job, he liked to say, proud of his own upkeep. Razor creases on his pants and resplendent white shirts were his trademarks. His generation had, after all, been weaned on the sartorial lunacy of the Jefe, who had owned just under ten thousand ties on the eve of his assassination. Dressed as he was, trim and serious, Papi looked foreign but not mojado.

That first day he chanced on a share in an apartment with three Guatemalans and his first job washing dishes at a Cuban sandwich shop. Once an old gringo diner of the hamburger and soda variety, the shop now filled with Óyemes and the aroma of lechón. Sandwich pressers clamped down methodically behind the front counter. The man reading the newspaper in the back told Papi he could start right away and gave him two white ankle-length aprons. Wash these every day, he said. We stay clean around here.

Two of Papi's apartment-mates were brothers, Stefan and Tomás Hernandez. Stefan was older than Tomás by twenty years. Both had families back home. Cataracts were slowly obscuring Stefan's eyes; the disease had cost him half a finger and his last job. He now swept floors and cleaned up vomit at the train station. This is a lot safer, he told my father. Working at a fabrica will kill you long before any tíguere will. Stefan had a passion for the track and would read the forms, despite his brother's warnings that he was ruining what was left of his eyes, by bringing his face down to the type. The tip of his nose was often capped in ink.

Eulalio was the third apartment-mate. He had the largest room to himself and owned the rusted-out Duster that brought them to work every morning. He'd been in the States close to two years and when he met Papi he spoke to him in English. When Papi didn't answer, Eulalio switched to Spanish. You're going to have to practice if you expect to get anywhere. How much English do you know?

None, Papi said after a moment.

Eulalio shook his head. Papi met Eulalio last and liked him least.

Papi slept in the living room, first on a carpet whose fraying threads kept sticking to his shaved head, and then on a mattress he salvaged from a neighbor. He worked two long shifts a day at the shop and had two four-hour breaks in between. On one of the breaks he slept at home and on the other he would handwash his aprons in the shop's sink and then nap in the storage room while the aprons dried, amidst the towers of El Pico coffee cans and sacks of bread. Sometimes he read the Western dreadfuls he was fond of – he could read one in about an hour. If it was too hot or he was bored by his book, he walked the neighborhoods, amazed at streets unblocked by sewage and the orderliness of the cars and houses. He was impressed with the transplanted Latinas, who had been transformed by good diets and beauty products unimagined back home. They were beautiful but unfriendly women. He would touch a finger to his beret and stop, hoping to slip in a comment or two, but these women would walk right on by, grimacing.

He wasn't discouraged. He began joining Eulalio on his

nightly jaunts to the bars. Papi would have gladly shared a drink with the Devil rather than go out alone. The Hernandez brothers weren't much for the outings; they were hoarders, though occasionally they cut loose, blinding themselves on tequila shots and beers. The brothers would stumble home late, stepping on Papi, howling about some morena who had spurned them to their faces.

Eulalio and Papi went out two, three nights a week, drinking rum and stalking. Whenever he could Papi let Eulalio do the buying. Eulalio liked to talk about the finca he had come from, a large plantation near the center of his country. I fell in love with the daughter of the owner and she fell in love with me. Me, a peon. Can you believe that? I would fuck her on her own mother's bed, in sight of the Holy Mother and her crucified Son. I tried to make her take down that cross but she wouldn't hear of it. She loved it that way. She was the one who lent me the money to come here. Can you believe that? One of these days, when I got a little money on the side I'm going to send for her.

It was the same story, seasoned differently, every night. Papi said little, believed less. He watched the women who were always with other men. After an hour or two, Papi would pay his bill and leave. Even though the weather was cool, he didn't need a jacket and liked to push through the breeze in shortsleeved shirts. He'd walk the mile home, talking to anyone who would let him. Occasionally drunkards would stop at his Spanish and invite him to a house where men and women were drinking and dancing. He liked those parties far better than the face-offs at the bars. It was with these strangers that he practiced his fledgling English, away from Eulalio's gleeful criticisms.

At the apartment, he'd lay down on his mattress, stretching out his limbs to fill it as much as he could. He abstained from thoughts of home, from thoughts of his two bellicose sons and the wife he had nicknamed Melao. He told himself, Think only of today and tomorrow. Whenever he felt weak, he'd take from under the couch the road map he bought at a gas station and trace his fingers up the coast, enunciating the city names slowly, trying to copy the awful crunch of sounds that was English. The northern coast of our Island was visible on the bottom right-hand corner of the map.

He left Miami in the winter. He'd lost his job and gained a new one but neither paid enough and the cost of the living-room floor was too great. Besides, Papi had figured out from a few calculations and from talking to the gringa downstairs (who now understood him) that Eulalio wasn't paying culo for rent. Which explained why he had so many fine clothes and didn't work nearly as much as the rest. When Papi showed the figures to the Hernandez brothers, written on the border of a newspaper, they were indifferent. He's the one with the car, they said, Stefan blinking at the numbers. Besides, who wants to start trouble here? We'll all be moving on anyway.

But this isn't right, Papi said. I'm living like a dog for this shit.

What can you do? Tomás said. Life smacks everybody around.

We'll see about that.

There are two stories about what happened next, one from Papi, one from Mami: either Papi left peacefully with a suitcase filled with Eulalio's best clothes or he beat the man first, and then took a bus and the suitcase to Virginia.

Papi logged most of the miles after Virginia on foot. He could have afforded another bus ticket but that would have bitten into the rent money he had so diligently saved on the advice of many a veteran immigrant. To be homeless in Nueva York was to court the worst sort of disaster. Better to walk three hundred and eighty miles than to arrive completely broke. He stored his savings in a fake alligator change purse he'd sewed into the seam of his boxer shorts. Though the purse blistered his thigh, it was in a place no thief would search.

He walked in his bad shoes, froze, and learned to distinguish different cars by the sounds of their motors. The cold wasn't as much a bother as his bags were. His arms ached from carrying them, especially the meat of his biceps. Twice he hitched rides from truckers who took pity on the shivering man and just outside of Delaware a K-car stopped him on the side of I-95.

These men were federal marshals. Papi recognized them immediately as police; he knew the type. He studied their car and considered running into the woods behind him. His visa had expired five weeks earlier and if caught, he'd go home in chains. He'd heard plenty of tales about the North American police from other illegals, how they liked to beat you before they turned you over to la migra and how sometimes they just took your money and tossed you out toothless on an abandoned road. For some reason, perhaps the whipping cold, perhaps stupidity, Papi stayed where he was, shuffling and sniffing. A window rolled down on the car. Papi went over and looked in on two sleepy blancos.

You need a ride?

Jes, Papi said.

The men squeezed together and Papi slipped into the front seat. Ten miles passed before he could feel his ass. When the chill and the roar of passing cars finally left him, he realized that a fragile-looking man, handcuffed and shackled, sat in the back seat. The small man wept quietly.

How far you going? the driver asked.

New York, he said, carefully omitting the Nueva.

We ain't going that far but you can ride with us to Trenton if you like. Where the hell you from, pal?

Miami.

Miami. Miami's kind of far from here. The other man looked at the driver. Are you a musician or something?

Jes, Papi said. I play the accordion.

That excited the man in the middle. Shit, my old man played the accordion but he was a Polack like me. I didn't know you spiks played it too. What kind of polkas do you like?

Polkas?

Jesus, Will, the driver said. They don't play accordions in Cuba.

They drove on, slowing only to unfold their badges at the tolls. Papi sat still and listened to the man crying in the back. What is wrong? Papi asked. Maybe sick?

The driver snorted. Him sick? We're the ones who are about to puke.

What's your name? the Polack asked.

Ramón.

136

Ramón, meet Scott Carlson Porter, murderer.

Murderer?

Many many murders. Mucho murders.

He's been crying since we left Georgia, the driver explained. He hasn't stopped. Not once. The little pussy cries even when we're eating. He's driving us nuts.

We thought maybe having another person inside with us would shut him up, the man next to Papi shook his head, but I guess not.

The marshals dropped Papi off in Trenton. He was so relieved not to be in jail that he didn't mind walking the four hours it took to summon the nerve to put his thumb out again.

His first year in Nueva York he lived in Washington Heights, in a roachy flat above what's now the Tres Marías restaurant. As soon as he secured his apartment and two jobs, one cleaning offices and the other washing dishes, he started writing home. In the first letter he folded four twenty-dollar bills. The trickles of money he sent back were not premeditated like those sent by his other friends, calculated from what he needed to survive; these were arbitrary sums that often left him broke and borrowing until the next payday.

The first year he worked nineteen-, twenty-hour days, seven days a week. Out in the cold he coughed, feeling as if his lungs were tearing open from the force of his exhales and in the kitchens the heat from the ovens sent pain corkscrewing into his head. He wrote home sporadically. Mami forgave him for what he had done and told him who else had left the barrio, via coffin or plane ticket. Papi's replies were scribbled on whatever he could find, usually the thin cardboard of tissue boxes or pages from the bill books at work. He was so tired from working that he misspelled almost everything and had to bite his lip to stay awake. He promised her and the children tickets soon. The pictures he received from Mami were shared with his friends at work and then forgotten in his wallet, lost between old lottery slips.

The weather was no good. He was sick often but was able to work through it and succeeded in saving up enough money to start looking for a wife to marry. It was the old routine, the oldest of the post-war maromas. Find a citizen, get married, wait, and then divorce her. The routine was well-practiced and expensive and riddled with swindlers.

A friend of his at work put him in touch with a portly balding blanco named el General. They met at a bar. El General had to eat two plates of greasy onion rings before he talked business. Look here friend, el General said. You pay me fifty bills and I bring you a woman that's interested. Whatever the two of you decide is up to you. All I care is that I get paid and that the women I bring are for real. You get no refunds if you can't work something out with her.

Why the hell don't I just go out looking for myself?

Sure, you can do that. He patted vegetable oil on Papi's hand. But I'm the one who takes the risk of running into Immigration. If you don't mind that then you can go out looking anywhere you want.

Even to Papi fifty bucks wasn't exorbitant but he was reluctant to part with it. He had no problem buying rounds at the bar or picking up a new belt when the colors and the moment suited him but this was different. He didn't want to deal with any more change. Don't get me wrong: it wasn't that he was having fun. No, he'd been robbed twice already, his ribs beaten until they were bruised. He often drank too much and went home to his room, and there he'd fume, spinning, angry at the stupidity that had brought him to this freezing hell of a country, angry that a man his age had to masturbate when he had a wife, and angry at the blinkered existence his jobs and the City imposed on him. He never had time to sleep, let alone to go to a concert or the museums that filled entire sections of the newspapers. And the roaches. The roaches were so bold in his flat that turning on the lights did not startle them. They waved their three-inch antennae as if to say, Hey puto, turn that shit off. He spent five minutes stepping on their carapaced bodies and shaking them from his mattress before dropping into his cot and still the roaches crawled on him at night. No, he wasn't having fun but he also wasn't ready to begin bringing his family over. Getting legal would place his hand firmly on that first rung. He wasn't so sure he could face us so soon. He asked his friends, most of who were in worse financial shape than he was, for advice.

They assumed he was reluctant because of the money. Don't be a pendejo, hombre. Give the fulano his money and that's it. Maybe you make good, maybe you don't. That's the way it is. They built these barrios out of bad luck and you got to get used to that.

He met el General across from the Boricua Cafeteria and handed him the money. A day later the man gave him a name: Flor de Oro. That isn't her real name of course, el General assured Papi. I like to keep things historical.

They met at the Cafeteria. Each of them had an empanada and a glass of soda. Flor was business-like, about fifty. Her gray hair coiled in a bun on top of her head. She smoked while Papi talked, her hands speckled like the shell of an egg.

Are you Dominican? Papi asked.

No.

You must be Cuban then.

One thousand dollars and you'll be too busy being an American to care where I'm from.

That seems like a lot of money. Do you think once I become a citizen I could make money marrying people?

I don't know.

Papi threw two dollars down on the counter and stood.

How much then? How much do you have?

I work so much that sitting here is like having a week's vacation. Still I only have six hundred.

Find two hundred more and we got a deal.

Papi brought her the money the next day stuffed in a wrinkled paper bag and in return was given a pink receipt. When do we get started? he asked.

Next week. I have to start on the paper work right away.

He pinned the receipt over his bed and before he went to sleep, he checked behind it to be sure no roaches lurked. His friends were excited and the boss at the cleaning job took them out for drinks and appetizers in Harlem, where their Spanish drew more looks than their frumpy clothes. Their excitement was not his; he felt as if he'd moved too precipitously. A week later, Papi went to see the friend who had recommended el General.

140

I still haven't gotten a call, he explained. The friend was scrubbing down a counter.

You will. The friend didn't look up. A week later Papi lay in bed, drunk, alone, knowing full well that he'd been robbed.

He lost the cleaning job shortly thereafter for punching the friend off a ladder. He lost his apartment and had to move in with a familia and found another job frying wings and rice at a Chinese take-out joint. Before he left his flat, he wrote an account of what had happened to him on the pink receipt and left it on the wall as a warning to whatever fool came next to take his place. Ten cuidado, he wrote. These people are worse than sharks.

He sent no money home for close to six months. Mami's letters would be read and folded and tucked into his well-used bags.

Papi met her on the morning before Christmas, in a laundry, while folding his pants and knotting his damp socks. She was short, had daggers of black hair pointing down in front of her ears and lent him her iron. She was originally from La Romana, but like so many Dominicans had eventually moved to the Capital.

I go back there about once a year, she told Papi. Usually around Pascua to see my parents and my sister.

I haven't been home in a long long time. I'm still trying to get the money together.

It will happen, believe me. It took me years before I could go back my first time.

Papi found out she'd been in the States for six years, a citizen. Her English was excellent. While he packed his things in his nylon bag, he considered asking her to the party. A friend had invited him to a house in Corona, Queens where fellow Dominicans were celebrating la Noche Buena together. He knew from a past party that up in Queens the food, dancing, and single women came in heaps.

Four children were trying to pry open the plate at the top of a dryer to reach the coin mechanism underneath. My fucking quarter is stuck, a kid was shouting. In the corner, a student, still in medical greens, was trying to read a magazine and not be noticed but as soon as the kids were tired of the machine, they descended on him, pulling at his magazine and pushing their hands into his pockets. He began to shove back.

Hey, Papi said. The kids threw him the finger and ran outside. Fuck all spiks! they shrieked.

Niggers, the medical student muttered. Papi pulled the drawstring shut on his bag and decided against asking her. He knew the rule: strange is the woman who goes strange places with a complete stranger. Instead, Papi asked her if he could practice his English on her one day. I really need to practice, he said. And I'd be willing to pay you for your time.

She laughed. Don't be ridiculous. Stop by when you can. She wrote her number and address in crooked letters.

Papi squinted at the paper. You don't live around here?

No but my cousin does. I can give you her number if you want.

No, this will be fine.

He had a grand time at the party and actually avoided the rum and the six-packs he liked to down. He sat with two older women and their husbands, a plate of food on his lap (potato salad, pieces of roast chicken, a stack of tostones, half an avocado, and a tiny splattering of mondongo out of politeness to the woman who'd brought it) and talked about his days in Santo Domingo. It was a lucid enjoyable night that would stick out in his memory like a spike. He swaggered home around one o'clock, bearing a plastic bag loaded with food and a loaf of telera under his arm. He gave the bread to the shivering man sleeping in the hallway of his building.

When he called Nilda a few days later he found out from a young girl who spoke in politely-spaced words that she was at work. Papi left his name and called back that night. Nilda answered.

Ramón, you should have called me yesterday. It was a good day to start since neither of us had work.

I wanted to let you celebrate the holiday with your family.

Family? She clucked. I only have a daughter here. What are you doing now? Maybe you want to come over.

I wouldn't want to intrude, he said because he was a sly one, you had to admit that.

She owned the top floor of a house on a bleak quiet street in Brooklyn. The house was clean, with cheap bubbled linoleum covering the floors. Nilda's taste struck Ramón as low-class. She threw together styles and colors the way a child might throw together paint or clay. A bright orange plaster elephant reared up from the center of a low glass table. A tapestry of a herd of mustangs hung opposite vinyl cutouts of African singers. Fake plants relaxed in each room. Her daughter Milagros was excruciatingly polite and seemed to have an endless supply of dresses more fit for quinceañeras than everyday life. She wore thick plastic glasses and sat in front of the television when Papi visited, one skinny leg crossed over the other. Nilda had a well-stocked kitchen and Papi cooked for her, his stockpile of Cantonese and Cuban recipes inexhaustible. His ropa vieja was his best dish and he was glad to see he had surprised her. I should have you in my kitchen, she said.

She liked to talk about the restaurant she owned and her last husband, who had a habit of hitting her and expecting that all his friends be fed for free. Nilda wasted hours of their study time caught between the leaves of tome-sized photo albums, showing Papi each stage of Milagros' development as if the girl were an exotic bug. He did not mention his own familia. Two weeks into his English lessons, Papi kissed Nilda. They were sitting on the plastic-covered sofa, in the next room a game show was on the TV, and his lips were greasy from Nilda's pollo guisado.

I think you better leave, she said.

You mean now?

Yes, now.

He drew on his windbreaker as slowly as he could, expecting her to recant. She held open the door and shut it swiftly. He cursed her the entire train ride back into Manhattan. The next day at work, he told his co-workers that she was insane and had a snake coiled up in her heart. A week later he was back at her house, grating coconuts and talking in English. He tried again and again she had him leave.

Each time he kissed her she threw him out. It was a cold winter and he didn't have much of a coat. Nobody bought coats then, Papi told me, because nobody was expecting to stay that long. So I kept going back and any chance I got I kissed her. She would tense up and tell me to leave, like I'd hit her. So I would kiss her again and she'd say, Oh, I really think you better leave now. She was a crazy lady. I kept it up and one day she kissed me back. Finally. By then I knew every maldito train in the city and I had this big wool coat and two pairs of gloves. I looked like an Eskimo. Like an American.

Within a month Papi moved out of his apartment into her house in Brooklyn. They were married in March.

Although he wore a ring, Papi didn't act the part of the husband. He lived in Nilda's house, shared her bed, paid no rent, ate her food, talked to Milagros when the TV was broken, and set up his weight bench in the cellar. He regained his health and liked to show Nilda how his triceps and biceps could gather in prominent knots with a twist of his arm. He bought his shirts in size medium so he could fill them out.

He worked at two jobs close to her house. The first soldering at a radiator shop, plugging holes mostly, the other as a cook at a Chinese restaurant. The owners of the restaurant were Chinese-Cubans; they cooked a better arroz negro than pork fried rice and loved to spend the quiet hours between lunch and dinner slapping dominos with Papi and the other help on top of huge drums of shortening. One day, while adding up his totals, Papi told these men about his familia in Santo Domingo.

The chief cook, a man so skinny they called him Needle, soured. You can't forget your familia like that. Didn't they support you to send you here?

I'm not forgetting them, Papi said defensively. Right

now is just not a good time for me to send for them. You should see my bills.

What bills?

Papi thought a moment. Electricity. That's very expensive. My house has eighty-eight light bulbs.

What kind of house are you living in?

Very big. An antique house needs a lot of bulbs, you know.

Come mierda. Nobody has that many light bulbs in their house.

You better do more playing and less talking or I'm going to have to take all your money.

These harangues must not have bothered his conscience much because that year he sent no money.

Nilda learned about Papi's other familia from a chain of friends that reached back across the Caribe. It was inevitable. She was upset and Papi had to deliver some of his most polished performances to convince her that he no longer cared about us. He'd been fortunate in that when Mami reached back across a similar chain of immigrants to locate Papi in the North, he'd told her to direct her letters to the restaurant he was working at and not to Nilda's home.

As with most of the immigrants around them, Nilda was usually at work. The couple saw each other mostly in the evenings. Nilda not only had her restaurant, where she served a spectacular and popular sancocho with wedges of cold avocado, but she also pushed her tailoring on the customers. If a man had a torn workshirt or a pant cuff soiled in machine oil, she'd tell him to bring it by, that she'd take care of it, cheap. She had a loud voice and could draw the attention of the entire eatery to a shabby article of clothing and few, under the combined gaze of their peers, could resist her. She brought the clothes home in a garbage bag and spent her time off sewing and listening to the radio, getting up only to bring Ramón a beer or change the channel for him. When she had to bring money home from the register, her skills at secreting it away were uncanny. She kept nothing but coins in her purse and switched her hiding place each trip. Usually she lined her bra with twenty-dollar bills as if each cup was a nest but Papi was amazed at her other ploys. After a crazy day of mashing platanos and serving the workers, she sealed nearly 900 dollars in twenties and fifties in a sandwich bag and then forced the bag into the mouth of a Malta bottle. She put a straw in there and sipped on it on her way home. She never lost a brown penny in the time she and Papi were together. If she wasn't too tired she liked to have him guess where she was hiding the money and with each wrong guess he'd remove a piece of her clothing until the cache was found.

Papi's best friend at this time, and Nilda's neighbor, was Jorge Carretas Lugones, or Jo-Jo as he was commonly known in the barrio. Jo-Jo was a five-foot-tall Puertorican whose light skin was stippled with moles and whose blue eyes were the color of larimar. In the street, he wore a pava, angled in the style of the past, carried a pen and all the local lotteries in his shirt pockets, and would have struck anyone as a hustler. Jo-Jo owned two hot dog carts and co-owned a grocery store that was very prosperous. It had once been a tired place with rotting wood and cracked tiles but with his two brothers he'd pulled the porquería out and rebuilt it over the four months of one winter, while driving a taxi and working as a translator and letter-writer for a local patron. The years of doubling the price on toilet paper, soap, and diapers to pay the loan sharks were over. The coffin refrigerators lining one wall were new, as were the bright green lottery machine and the revolving racks of junk food at the end of each short shelf. He was disdainful of anyone who had a regular crowd of parasites loafing about their stores, discussing the taste of yuca and their last lays. And though this neighborhood was rough (not as bad as his old barrio in San Juan where he had seen all his best friends lose fingers in machete fights), Jo-Jo didn't need to put a grate over his store. The local kids left him alone and instead terrorized a Pakistani family down the street. The family owned an Asian grocery store that looked like a holding cell, windows behind steel mesh, door reinforced with steel plates.

Jo-Jo and Papi met at the local bar regularly. Papi was the man who knew the right times to laugh and when he did everyone around him joined in. He was always reading newspapers and sometimes books and seemed to know many things. Jo-Jo saw in Papi another brother, a man from a luckless past needing a little direction. Jo-Jo had already rehabilitated two of his siblings, who were on their way to owning their own stores.

Now that you have a place and papers, Jo-Jo told Papi, you need to use these things to your advantage. You have some time, you don't have to break your ass paying the rent, so use it. Save some money and buy yourself a little business. I'll sell you one of my hot dog carts cheap if you want. You can see they're making steady plata. Then you get your familia over here and buy yourself a nice house and start branching out. That's the American way.

Papi wanted a negocio of his own, that was his dream, but he balked at starting at the bottom, selling hot dogs. While most of the men around him were two-times broke, he had seen a few, fresh off the boat, shake the water from their backs and jump right into the lowest branches of the American establishment. That leap was what he envisioned for himself, not some slow upward crawl through the mud. What it would be and when it would come, he did not know.

I'm looking for the right investment, he told Jo-Jo. I'm not a food man.

What sort of man are you then? Jo-Jo demanded. Dominicans got restaurants in their blood.

I know, Papi said, but I am not a food man.

Worse, Jo-Jo spouted a hard line on loyalty to familia which troubled Papi. Each scenario his friend proposed ended with Papi's familia living safely within his sight, showering him with love. Papi had difficulty separating the two threads of his friend's beliefs, that of negocios and that of familia, and in the end the two became impossibly intertwined.

With the hum of his new life Papi should have found it easy to bury the memory of his first familia but neither his conscience, nor the letters from home that found him wherever he went, would allow it. Mami's letters, as regular as the months themselves, were corrosive slaps in the face. It was now a one-sided correspondence, with Papi reading and not mailing anything back. He opened the letters wincing in anticipation. Mami detailed how his children were suffering, how his littlest boy was so anemic people thought he was a corpse come back to life; she told him about his oldest son, playing in the barrio, tearing open his feet and exchanging blows with his so-called friends. Mami refused to talk about her condition. She called Papi a desgraciado and a puto of the highest order for abandoning them, a traitor worm, an eater of pubic lice, a cockless, ball-less cabrón. He showed Jo-Jo the letters, often at drunken bitter moments, and Jo-Jo would shake his head, waving for two more beers. You, my compadre, have done too many things wrong. If you keep this up, your life will spring apart.

What in the world can I do? What does this woman want from me? I've been sending her money. Does she want me to starve up here?

You and I know what you have to do. That's all I can say, otherwise I'd be wasting my breath.

Papi was lost. He would take long perilous night walks home from his jobs, sometimes arriving with his knuckles scuffed and his clothes disheveled. His and Nilda's child was born in the spring, a son, also named Ramón, cause for fiesta but there was no celebration among his friends. Too many of them knew. Nilda could sense that something was wrong, that a part of him was detained elsewhere but each time she brought it up Papi told her it was nothing, always nothing.

With a regularity that proved instructional, Jo-Jo had Papi drive him to Kennedy International to meet one or the other of the relatives Jo-Jo had sponsored to come to the States to make it big. Despite his prosperity, Jo-Jo could not drive and did not own a car. Papi would borrow Nilda's Chevy station wagon and would fight the traffic for an hour to reach the airport. Depending on the season, Jo-Jo would bring either a number of coats or a cooler of beverages taken from his shelves – a rare treat since Jo-Jo's cardinal rule was that one should never prey on one's own stock. At the terminal, Papi would stand back, his hands pressed in his pockets, his beret plugged on tight, while Jo-Jo surged forward to greet his familia. Papi's English was good now, his clothes better. Jo-Jo would enter a berserk frenzy when his relatives stumbled through the arrival gate, dazed and grinning, bearing cardboard boxes and canvas bags. There would be crying and abrazos. Jo-Jo would introduce Ramón as a brother and Ramón would be dragged into the circle of crying people. It was a simple matter for Ramón to rearrange the faces of the arrivals and see his wife and his children there.

He began again to send money to his familia on the Island. Nilda noticed that he began to borrow from her for his tobacco and to play the lotteries. Why do you need my money? she complained. Isn't that the reason you're working? We have a baby to look after. There are bills to pay.

One of my children died, he said. I have to pay for the wake and the funeral. So leave me alone.

Why didn't you tell me?

He put his hands over his face but when he removed them she was still staring skeptically.

Which one? she demanded. His hand swung clumsily. She fell down and neither of them said a word.

Papi landed a union job with Reynolds Aluminum in West New York that paid triple what he was making at the radiator shop. It was nearly a two-hour commute, followed by a day of tendon-ripping labor, but he was willing – the money and the benefits were exceptional. It was the first time he had moved outside the umbra of his fellow immigrants. The racism was pronounced. The two fights he had were reported to the bosses and they put him on probation. He worked through that period, got a raise and the highest performance rating in his department and the shittiest schedule in the entire fabrica. The whites were always dumping their bad shifts on him and on his friend Chuito. Guess what, they'd say, clapping them on the back. I need a little time with my kids this week. I know you wouldn't mind taking this or that day for me.

No, my friend, Papi would say. I wouldn't mind. Once Chuito complained to the bosses and was written up for detracting from the familial spirit of the department. Both men knew better than to speak up again.

On a normal day Papi was too exhausted to visit with Jo-Jo. He'd enjoy his dinner and then settle down to watch Tom and Jerry, who delighted him with their violence and their resilience. Nilda, watch this, he'd scream and she'd dutifully appear, needles in mouth, baby in her arms. Papi would laugh so loud that Milagros upstairs would join in without even seeing what had occurred. Oh, that's wonderful, he'd say. Would you look at that! They're killing each other!

One day, he skipped his dinner and a night in front of the TV to drive south with Chuito into New Jersey to a small town outside of Perth Amboy. Chuito's Gremlin pulled into a neighborhood under construction. Huge craters had been gouged in the earth and towering ziggurats of tan bricks stood ready to be organized into buildings. New pipes were being laid by the mile and the air was tart with the smell of chemicals. It was a cool night. The men wandered around the pits and the sleeping trucks.

I have a friend who is doing the hiring for this place, Chuito said.

Construction?

No. When this neighborhood goes up they'll need superintendents to watch over things. Keep the hot water running, stop a leaking faucet, put a new tile in the bathroom. For that you get a salary and free rent. That's the kind of job worth having. The towns nearby are quiet, lots of good gringos. Listen Ramón, I can get you a job here if you like. It would be a good place to move. Out of the city, safety. I'll put your name at the top of the list and when this place is done you'll have a nice easy job.

This sounds better than a dream.

Forget dreams. This is real, compadre.

The two men inspected the site for about an hour and then headed back to Perth Amboy. Papi was silent. A plan was forming. Here was the place to move his familia if it came from the Island. Quiet and close to his job. Most important, the neighborhood would not know him or the wife he had in the States. When he reached home that night he said nothing to Nilda about where he had been. He didn't care that she was suspicious and that she yelled at him about his muddy shoes.

Papi continued to send money home and in Jo-Jo's lock box he was saving a tidy sum for plane tickets. And then one morning, when the sun had taken hold of the entire house and the sky seemed too thin and blue to hold a cloud, Nilda said, I want to go to the Island this year.

Are you serious?

I want to see my viejos.

153

What about the baby?

He's never gone, has he?

No.

Then he should see his patria. I think it's important.

I agree, he said. He tapped a pen on the wrinkled place-mat. This sounds like you're serious.

I think I am.

Maybe I'll go with you.

If you say so. She had reason to doubt him; he was real good at planning but real bad at doing. And she didn't stop doubting him either, until he was on the plane next to her, rifling anxiously through the catalogs, the vomit bag, and the safety instructions.

He was in Santo Domingo for five days. He stayed at Nilda's familia's house on the western edge of the city. It was painted bright orange with an outhouse slumped nearby and a pig pushing around in a pen. Homero and Josefa, tíos of Nilda, drove home with them from the airport in a cab and gave them the 'bedroom.' The couple slept in the other room, the 'living room.'

Are you going to see them? Nilda asked that first night. They were both listening to their stomachs struggling to digest the heaping meal of yuca and higado they had eaten. Outside, the roosters were pestering each other.

Maybe, he said. If I get the time.

I know that's the only reason you're here.

What's wrong with a man seeing his familia? If you had to see your first husband for some reason, I'd let you, wouldn't I?

Does she know about me?

154

Of course she knows about you. Not like it matters now. She's out of the picture completely.

She didn't answer him. He listened to his heart beating, and began to sense its slick contours.

On the plane, he'd been confident. He'd talked to the vieja near the aisle, telling her how excited he was. It is always good to return home, she said tremulously. I come back anytime I can, which isn't so much any more. Things aren't good. Seeing the country he'd been born in, seeing his people in charge of everything, he was unprepared for it. The air whooshed out of his lungs. For nearly four years he'd not spoken his Spanish loudly in front of the North Americans and now he was hearing it bellowed and flung from every mouth.

His pores opened, dousing him as he hadn't been doused in years. An awful heat was on the city and the red dust dried out his throat and clogged his nose. The poverty – the unwashed children pointing sullenly at his new shoes, the familias slouching in hovels – was familiar and stifling.

He felt like a tourist, riding a guagua to Boca Chica and having his and Nilda's photograph taken in front of the Alcazar de Colón. He was obliged to eat two or three times a day at various friends of Nilda's familia; he was, after all, the new successful husband from the North. He watched Josefa pluck a chicken, the wet plumage caking her hands and plastering the floor, and remembered the many times he'd done the same, up in Santiago, his first home, where he no longer belonged.

He tried to see his familia but each time he set his mind to it, his resolve scattered like leaves before a hurricane wind. Instead he saw his old friends on the force and drank six bottles of Brugal in three days. Finally, on the fourth day of his visit, he borrowed the nicest clothes he could find and folded two hundred dollars into his pocket. He took a guagua down Sumner Welles, as Calle XXI had been renamed, and cruised into the heart of his old barrio. Colmados on every block and billboards plastering every exposed wall or board. The children chased each other with hunks of cinder block from nearby buildings – a few threw rocks at the guagua, the loud pings jerking the passengers upright. The progress of the guagua was frustratingly slow, each stop seemed spaced four feet from the last. Finally, he disembarked, walking two blocks to the corner of XXI and Tunti. The air must have seemed thin then, and the sun like a fire in his hair, sending trickles of sweat down his face. He must have seen people he knew. Jayson sitting glumly at his colmado, a soldier turned grocer. Chicho, gnawing at a chicken bone while at his feet a row of newly-shined shoes. Maybe Papi stopped there and couldn't go on, maybe he went as far as the house, which hadn't been painted since his departure. Maybe he even stopped at our house and stood there, waiting for his children out front to recognize him.

In the end, he never visited us. If Mami heard from her friends that he was in the city, with his other wife, she never told us about it. His absence was a seamless thing to me. And if a strange man approached me during my play and stared down at me and my siblings, perhaps asking our names, I don't remember it now.

Papi returned home and had trouble resuming his routine. He took a couple of sick days, the first ever, and spent the time in front of the television and at the bar. Twice he turned down negocios from Jo-Jo. The first ended in utter failure, cost Jo-Jo 'the gold in his teeth,' but the FOB clothing store on Smith Street, with the bargain basement buys, the enormous bins of factory seconds and a huge layaway shelf, pulled in the money in bags. Papi had recommended the location to Jo-Jo, having heard about the vacancy from Chuito, who was still living in Perth Amboy. London Terrace Apartments had not yet opened.

After work Papi and Chuito caroused in the bars on Smith and Elm Streets and every few nights Papi stayed over in Perth Amboy. Nilda had continued to put on weight after the birth of the third Ramón and while Papi favored heavy women, he didn't favor obesity and wasn't inclined to go home. Who needs a woman like you? he told her. The couple began to fight on a regular schedule. Locks were changed, doors were broken, slaps were exchanged but weekends and an occasional weekday night were still spent together.

In the dead of summer, when the potato-scented fumes from the diesel forklifts were choking the warehouses, Papi was helping another man shove a crate into position when he felt a twinge about midway up his spine. Hey asshole, keep pushing, the other man grunted. Pulling his work shirt out of his Dickies, Papi twisted to the right, then to the left and that was it, something snapped. He fell to his knees. The pain was so intense, shooting through him like fireballs from Roman candles, that he vomited on the concrete floor of the warehouse. His co-workers moved him to the lunch room. For two hours he tried repeatedly to walk and failed. Chuito came down from his division, concerned for his friend but also worried that this unscheduled break would piss off his boss. How are you? he asked.

Not so good. You have to get me out of here.

You know I can't leave.

Then call me a cab. Just get me home. Like anyone wounded, he thought home could save him.

Chuito called him the taxi; none of the other employees took time to help him walk out.

Nilda put him in bed and had a cousin to manage the restaurant. Jesú, he moaned to her. I should've slowed down a little. Just a little bit longer and I would've been home with you. Do you know that? A couple of hours more.

She went down to the botánica for a poultice and then down to the bodega for aspirin. Let's see how well the old magic works, she said, smearing the poultice onto his back.

For two days he couldn't move, not even his head. He ate very little, strictly soups she concocted. More than once he fell asleep and woke up to find Nilda out, shopping for medicinal teas, and Milagros over him, a grave owl in her large glasses. Mi hija, he said. I feel like I'm dying.

You won't die, she said.

And what if I do?

Then Mama will be alone.

He closed his eyes and prayed that she would be gone and when he opened them, she was and Nilda was coming in through the door with another remedy, steaming on a battered tray.

He was able to sit up and call in sick by himself on the fourth day. He told the morning shift manager that he couldn't move too well. I think I stay in bed, he said. The manager told him to come in so he could receive a medical furlough. Papi had Milagros find the name of a lawyer in the phone book. He was thinking law suit. He had dreams, fantastic dreams of gold rings and a spacious house with caged tropical birds in its rooms, a house awash with sea winds. The woman lawyer he contacted only worked divorces but she gave him the name of her brother.

Nilda wasn't optimistic about his plan. Do you think the gringo will part with his money like that? The reason they're so pale is because they're terrified of not having any plata. Have you even spoken to the man you were helping? He's probably going to be a witness for the company so that he won't lose his job the same way you're going to lose yours. That maricón will probably get a raise for it, too.

I'm not an illegal, he said. I'm protected.

I think it's better if you let it drop.

He called Chuito to sound him out. Chuito wasn't optimistic either. The boss knows what you're trying to yank. He no like it, compadre. He say you better get back to work or you're quitted.

His courage failing, Papi started pricing a consultation with an independent doctor. Very likely, his father's foot was hopping about in his mind. His father, José Edilio, the loud-mouthed ball-breaking vagrant who had never married Papi's mother but nevertheless had given her nine children, had attempted a similar stunt when he worked in a hotel kitchen in Río Piedras. José had accidently dropped a tin of stewed tomatoes on his foot. Two small bones broke but instead of seeing a doctor, José kept working, limping around the kitchen. Every day at work, he'd smile at his fellow workers and say, I guess it's time to take care of that foot. Then he'd smash another can on it, figuring the worse it was, the more money he'd get when he finally showed the bosses. It saddened and shamed Papi to hear of this while he was growing up. The old man was rumored to have wandered the barrio he lived in, trying to find someone who would take a bat to the foot. For the old man that foot was an investment, an heirloom he cherished and burnished, until half of it had to be amputated because the infection was so bad.

After another week and with no calls from the lawyers, Papi saw the company doctor. His spine felt as if there was broken glass inside of it but he was given three weeks of medical leave by the company doctor. Ignoring the instructions on the medication he swallowed ten pills a day for the pain. He got better. When he returned to the job he could work and that was enough. The bosses were unanimous, however, in voting down Papi's next raise. They demoted him to the rotating shift he'd been on during the first days of the job.

Instead of taking his licks, he blamed it on Nilda. Puta was what he took to calling her. They fought with renewed vigor; the orange elephant was knocked over and lost a tusk. She kicked him out twice but after probationary weeks at Jo-Jo's allowed him to return. He saw less of his son, avoiding all of the daily routines that fed and maintained the infant. The third Ramón was a handsome child who roamed the house restlessly, tilted forward and at full speed, as if he were a top that had been sent spinning. Papi was good at playing with the baby, pulling him by his foot across the floor and tickling his sides, but as soon as the third Ramón started to fuss, playtime was over. Nilda, come and tend to this, he'd say.

The third Ramón resembled Papi's other sons and on occasion he'd say, Yunior, don't do that. If Nilda heard these slips she would explode. Maldito, she'd cry, picking up the child and retreating with Milagros into the bedroom. Papi didn't screw up too often but he was never certain how many times he'd called the third Ramón with the second son Ramón in mind.

With his back killing him and his life with Nilda headed down the toilet, Papi began more and more to regard his departure as inevitable. His first familia was the logical destination. He began to see them as his saviors, as a regenerative force that could redeem his fortunes. He said as much to Jo-Jo. Now you're finally talking sense, panín, Jo-Jo said. Chuito's imminent departure from the warehouse also emboldened Ramón to act. London Terrace Apartments, delayed because of a rumor that it had been built on a chemical dump site, had finally opened.

Jo-Jo was only able to promise Papi half the money he needed. Jo-Jo was still throwing away money on his failed negocio and needed a little time to recover. Papi took this as a betrayal and said so to their friends. He talks a big game but when you're at the final inning, you get nada. Although these accusations filtered back to Jo-Jo and wounded him, he still loaned Papi the money without comment. That's how Jo-Jo was. Papi worked for the rest of it, more months than he expected. Chuito reserved him an apartment and together they began filling the place with furniture. He started taking a shirt or two with him to work, which he then sent to the apartment. Sometimes he'd cram socks in his pockets or put on two pairs of underwear. He was smuggling himself out of Nilda's life.

What's happening to your clothes? she asked one night.

It's that damn cleaners, he said. That bobo keeps losing my things. I'm going to have to have a word with him as soon I get a day off.

Do you want me to go?

I can handle this. He's a very nasty guy.

The next morning she caught him cramming two guayaberas in his lunch pail. I'm sending these two to be cleaned, he explained.

Let me do them.

You're too busy. It's easier this way.

He wasn't very smooth about it.

They spoke only when necessary.

Years later Nilda and I would speak, after he had left us for good, after her children had moved out of the house. Milagros had children of her own and their pictures crowded on tables and walls. Nilda's son loaded baggage at JFK airport. I picked up the picture of him with his girlfriend. We were brothers all right though his face respected symmetry.

We sat in the kitchen, in that same house, and listened to the occasional pop of a rubber ball being batted down the wide channel between the building fronts. My mother had given me her address (Give my regards to the puta, she'd said) and I'd taken three trains to reach her, walked blocks with her address written on my palm.

I'm Ramón's son, I'd said.

Hijo, I know who you are.

She fixed café con leche and offered me a Goya cracker.

162

No thanks, I said, no longer as willing to ask her questions or even to be sitting there. Anger has a way of returning. I looked down at my feet and saw that the linoleum was worn and filthy. Her hair was white and cut close to her small head. We sat and drank and finally talked, two strangers reliving an event – a whirlwind, a comet, a war – we'd both seen but from different faraway angles.

He left in the morning, she explained quietly. I knew something was wrong because he was lying in bed, not doing anything but stroking my hair, which was very long back then. I was a Pentecostal. Usually he didn't lay around in bed. As soon as he was awake he was showered and dressed and gone. He had that sort of energy. But when he got up he just stood over little Ramón. Are you OK? I asked him and he said he was just fine. I wasn't going to fight with him about it so I went right back to sleep. The dream I had is one I still think about. I was young and it was my birthday and I was eating a plate of quail's eggs and all of them were for me. A silly dream really. When I woke up I saw that the rest of his things were gone.

She cracked her knuckles slowly. I thought that I would never stop hurting. I knew then what it must have been like for your mother. You should tell her that.

We talked until it got dark and then I got up. Outside the local kids were gathered in squads, stalking in and out of the lucid clouds produced by the street lamps. She suggested I go to her restaurant but when I got there and stared through my reflection in the glass at the people inside, all of them versions of people I already knew, I decided to go home.

December. He had left in December. The company had given him a two-week vacation, which Nilda knew nothing about. He drank a cup of black café in the kitchen and left it washed and drying in the caddy. I doubt if he was crying or even anxious. He lit a cigarette, tossed the match on the kitchen table and headed out into the angular winds that were blowing long and cold from the south. He ignored the convoys of empty cabs that prowled the streets and walked down Atlantic. There were less furniture and antique shops then. He smoked cigarette after cigarette and killed his pack within the hour. He bought a carton at a stand, knowing how expensive they would be abroad.

The first subway station on Bond would have taken him to the airport and I like to think that he grabbed that first train, instead of what was more likely true, that he had gone out to Chuito's first, before flying south to get us.

Glossary

abrazo	an embrace
abuelo	grandfather
aguantando	enduring, waiting
askho	disgust
barrio	neighborhood
bobo	a dope
botánica	shop selling spritual items, cures, divinations
cabrón	a cuckold
campo	the countryside
carajo	a curse
casas ajenas	strange houses
cojones	balls
colmado	a small general store/bar
come mierda	a shit-eater
¿como te sientas?	how are you feeling?
coño	a curse
Dios mio	my God
¿entiendes?	understand?
fabrica	factory
flaca	a skinny woman or girl
flojo	loose
FOB	fresh-off-the-boat
fulano	Tom, Dick and Harry all balled into one
guagua	a bus
guayabera	an embroidered shirt

hija, hijo	daughter, son
hombres de negocios	businessman
jurone	mongoose
malcriado	badly raised
maldito	damned
muchacho	kid
nalgas	ass
negocios	a business or negotiation
ojo	eyes
olvidate	forget about it
Óyeme	listen to me
pato	a queer
pava	a traditional hat
pendejo	a pussy or a punk
ponchera	basin
porquería	filth or junk
puta, puto	bitch or whore, male or female
Quisqueya	Taino Indian name for the Dominican Republic
sancocho	a stew
santera, santero	a spiritual worker
sinvergüenza	one without shame
sucia	a tramp
tía, tío	aunt, uncle
tígueres	street kids or straight-up hoods
vaina	shit
vieja, viejo	old woman, old man
zángano	an about-nothing person